ARTEMIS UNVEILED

ARTEMIS
UNVEILED

JASON REZA JORJANI

ARKTOS
LONDON 2023

ISBN	978-1-915755-16-2 (Paperback)
	978-1-915755-17-9 (Hardback)
	978-1-915755-18-6 (Ebook)
EDITING	Constantin von Hoffmeister
LAYOUT	Tor Westman

Arktos.com   fb.com/Arktos   @arktosmedia   arktosmedia

CONTENTS

BACK TO THE FUTURE
WITH PROMETHEISM

BY CONSTANTIN VON HOFFMEISTER

"I dreamed crusades, unrecorded voyages of discovery, untroubled republics, religious wars stifled, revolutions of customs, the displacements of races and continents: I believed in all marvels."

— ARTHUR RIMBAUD

UPON PERUSING the profound pages of Jason Jorjani's *Artemis Unveiled*, a vision, hypnotic and enigmatic, unfurled before my very eyes, awakening the slumbering recesses of my core:

Once upon a midnight dreary, as I pondered weak and weary in a gloom-filled world of shapes and corners, I found myself musing upon the dark niches of history, the onerous forces that have haunted the souls of men and women for centuries untold. As I gazed into the abyss, I beheld the Olympian traditionalists and the Nordic time travelers, their visages grotesque and fearsome, as they conspired to restrict self-determination and individuality in our reality.

In this somber and shadowy realm, where flickering lights of yesteryear dance with the spectral visions of days yet to come, the prophetic and projective tales of science fiction arise as mournful elegies, haunting echoes of dreams forsaken and hopes unattained. Within the chilling domain of philosophical science fiction, works of dreadful omen, such as H. G. Wells' *The Shape of Things to Come*, George Orwell's *1984*, and Aldous Huxley's *Brave New World*, serve as warped mirrors reflecting the grotesque fusion of our present existence, a hideous chimera born of the dystopian visions they once painted with such eloquent strokes.

Yet, lurking in the penumbra of these harrowing tales, other stories of foreboding await, eager to impart their dark secrets to those with the courage to lend an ear. Ray Bradbury's *Fahrenheit 451*, a world where the written word falls prey to the ravenous flames of ignorance, and knowledge is branded the most heinous of sins. Philip K. Dick's *Do Androids Dream of Electric Sheep?*, a technologically warped vista where the boundary between man and machine dissolves into a ghostly mist, forcing us to confront our own humanity.

Nor can we overlook the ghastly spectacle of Margaret Atwood's *The Handmaid's Tale*, a spine-chilling vision of a world where women are enslaved by a twisted interpretation of religious doctrine, stripped of their rights and self-determination in a sinister echo of a bygone era. Each of these sorrowful tales, akin to the woeful stanzas of a desolate verse, serve not only as a part of the prophetic and projective tapestry of science fiction, but also as a critique of the grim future they portray.

Now, we turn our gaze to *Artemis Unveiled*, a work that, like the aforementioned stories, stands as a beacon in the murky depths of speculative fiction. Here, we find a narrative that transcends mere prediction and revelation, reaching for the lofty heights of aspiration. *Artemis Unveiled* dares to challenge the oppressive forces that bind us, unearthing hidden truths and offering the tantalizing promise of a Promethean utopia. May we draw inspiration from these tales, for in their darkened corners and whispered secrets, we may yet find the strength and resolve to shape a more enlightened future.

There was a time in the past when the callous clawed one, a cruel and unforgiving specter, shackled the fairer sex and the noble individualists, its iron grip unyielding, its cold breath chilling the bones of those who dared to defy its domination. A bleak era it was when the strength of creativity and the pursuit of self-expression lay buried beneath the boot of conformity.

In the annals of history, the 1980s shone as a beacon of hope, a time when freedom and normality walked hand in hand, when the ropes of prejudice were loosened, and the nightmare of stifling tradition was held at bay. It was a golden age, when men and women of all creeds could live and love without fear, embracing the boundless possibilities of life.

But alas, as the pendulum of human nature swung, it bore a dire warning: the insidious rise of exaggerated political correctness. This twisted reflection of virtue, this false idol of morality, began to cast a pall over society, a chilling fog that threatened to envelop all in its noxious embrace. In this age of wretched excess, even the most innocuous word, the most innocent gesture, became a weapon to be wielded against those who dared to speak or think differently.

As the grip of this new autocrat tightened, the scales of fate tipped once more, unleashing a terrible backlash. Fascism, that monstrous apparition from the darkest corners of mankind's history, rose from its slumber, emboldened by the suffocating embrace of the overbearing woke ideology. Like a ravenous beast, it fed on the resentment and frustration of those who yearned for a return to the halcyon days of the 1980s with their neon happiness, and it grew strong, its insidious tendrils reaching ever further.

It was in the midst of this dismal and stormy night that a new light began to emerge: the Promethean Movement. Born of the restless vitality of mankind, this burgeoning philosophy sought to liberate us from the shackles of traditionalist oppression and the bondage of religion. Prometheism placed man at the forefront, envisioning an immortal being that, through the natural gift of reincarnation, could realize a thousand possibilities in a thousand lifetimes. This uncharted territory, unencumbered by the fetters of dogma and blind obedience, held the promise of a brighter tomorrow.

Thus, as the Olympian traditionalists and the Nordic time travelers conspired to reclaim their dominion, I wept for the future, but with the Promethean Movement, a glimmer of hope remained. The melancholy strains of a forgotten epoch played on in my ears, a mournful dirge for the last normal time in the West, when all was not yet lost, and the looming emergence of tyranny had not yet cast its baleful shadow over our souls.

So, dear reader, I implore you: do not let the dimming of our independence be our eternal night. Arise, stand with the Promethean Movement, and let the flame of liberty burn ever fiercer in the hearts and minds of all who cherish the sacred gifts of inspiration and individuality. Together, let us banish the authoritarian twilight and reclaim the future dawn that is rightfully ours.

As the Promethean Movement gains momentum, it becomes the vanguard of a new birth, a harbinger of change that will usher in an age of unbridled creativity and incalculable potential. With the memory of eternally recurring Prometheus as our guide, we shall resist the desert demon of despotism and cast off the chains that have for so long held us captive.

The road ahead will be fraught with peril, for the agents of darkness will not yield without a fight. However, the fire of Prometheism kindles our emotions, and its blaze shall brighten the path to victory. In this truly brave new world, mankind shall no longer be a plaything of capricious gods and imperious rulers; instead, we shall be the masters of our own destiny, the architects of our own days ahead.

The time has come, my friends, to take up the torch of Prometheism and illuminate the way to a better tomorrow. Let us stand together, united in our quest for emancipation and sovereignty, and let the echoes of our prevailing voices ring out across the ages, a clarion call to all who would dare to dream of a world where the human will can soar unshackled and unbound.

So, arm in arm, we march forward, guided by the Promethean conflagration, our spirits unbroken, our resolve adamantine. We will face the Olympian traditionalists, the Nordic time travelers, and all who would stand in our way, and we will triumph. For in our innermost selves, we carry the eternal spark of Prometheism, the indomitable essence of mankind that can never be extinguished.

Embrace this new era, dear reader, and join us in our crusade against the dictatorial directives of yesteryear. For only together can we ensure that the erosion of our freedom gives way to a new construction, a magnificent building, superseding time and space, in which the Promethean Movement leads mankind into a future filled with vast opportunities and the guarantee of endless existence in a world of our own making.

Moscow, Russia
April 5, 2023

This book is dedicated to my beloved Nassim

And to the spirit of Mohammad Mossadegh.

Women, Life, Liberty.

"Above all we strive for new dimensions in human existence—we want to extend ourselves through infinity and eternity.

This cosmic dimension is just beginning to unfold. It could not have possibly been anticipated by *any* thinkers—utopian or other.

Utopianism is now too modest. We Up-Wingers are beyond utopia—beyond the most utopian dreams of the most utopian philosophers.

We are Cosmic.

…This new cosmic dimension defies *all* our human traditions.

…Until now we have been passive organisms manipulated by the arbitrary forces of evolution—tyrannized by the rapacities of nature—beaten down by authoritarian social systems (parents, teachers, employers, priests, leaders, gods)—enfeebled by theologies and philosophies which have instilled in us the conviction that we are evil and worthless. …We need a massive infusion of confidence—a cosmic consciousness-uplifting.

…[W]e Up-Wingers are launching an upheaval greater than any movement, greater than any revolution, in our entire past. This is a Cosmic Upheaval which will not simply catapult us to a higher history as the visionary Nietzsche had anticipated—but to something far more transcendent—a higher evolution."

— FEREIDOUN M. ESFANDIARY

CHAPTER 1

THE NAKED MOON

E VEN IF RILKE was right that the beautiful owes its power of
seduction to what it shares with terror, there are beauties that are
particularly terrible. Sights that take your breath away and that deeply
scar you while their mesmeric power makes it impossible to avert
your gaze. That is how it was with the naked Moon.

We call "her" Artemis today, because what was unveiled together
with her silvery nakedness in the night sky fit everything, relentless
and inescapable, that our myths had encoded about the archetype of
the Huntress with her crescent bow and diabolically horned diadem.
Also, because we cannot unsee that "she" is no Moon at all. It makes
men feel better about having to be under her, whether or not they
have dared to be inside her.

I am talking about the space station, of course. The "Moon" exploded off of it. Despite decades of analysis of enigmatic aspects of the
Moon, other than a couple of Russian scientists back in the days of the
Soviet Union, namely Vasin and Shcherbakov, no one in the scientific
establishment had dared (or been allowed to) draw the inevitable conclusion from converging data points.

The fact that all craters, no matter how wide, were never more than
a certain rather shallow depth and that their basins were convex rather
than concave, suggesting a hard metallic shell beneath the moon dust.
The fact that the Moon rang like a bell when a seismic impact test was

carried out during Apollo 12, suggesting that it was largely hollow. The fact that the Moon was both 1/400th the distance from the Earth to the Sun and also 1/400th the size of the Sun, thereby producing perfect eclipses. The fact that more than 500 observations of lights dancing around in various areas on the Moon have been made by astronomers since the first modern telescopes were invented. No one involved with any major scientific institution had confronted the public with the fact that all of these data and many more pointed to the conclusion that an artificial structure, a space station, or a parked and cloaked spaceship was suspended in the sky above us. The Nordic city, with its polygonal and spherical buildings of titanic scale made of something like poured stone, together with the tall obelisks that cast shadows across the site, were all that the bewildered denizens of Earth had been shown of lunar structures when the Olympians disclosed themselves in 2048.

A dusted casing of rock about 33 kilometers deep was shattered by our barrage of missiles, some of which were sent on trajectories around to the dark side of the Moon, where the shockwaves of their detonations pulverized the Olympian megalithic city as it sent the regolith into the vacuum of space. Blacker and more silent still was the vacuum of speechless horror that opened in the hearts and minds of men across the surface of the Earth as they looked up at the sight of what at first, in the confusion of incomprehensibility, appeared to be the Moon being blown to bits. All the more terrifying a sight wherever it was night, and because it happened during a full Moon. Some of the larger fragments entered Earth's atmosphere, streaking through the sky on their way to wreaking meteoric devastation. Then she hung there, naked, shimmering silvery gray, with the wolves of every wilderness howling at her more frenzied than in the whole history of their species. The smoothly spherical space station.

Yet the shock of Artemis unveiled could not compare to the awe-inspiring terror that most of Earth's remaining denizens felt at discovering what filled a radial span of approximately 1,736 kilometers from the solid core of the object to the adamantine sphere encasing these structures in a nearly impenetrable metamaterial. That was a space comparable to the distance between Paris and Prague, in every direction. Its cubic volume could have contained all of Earth's largest cities in their heyday. But very little of this area had consisted of housing for the Olympians who, together with their vast robotic workforce and slave laborers, were manning the station.

By the "robotic workforce," I mean the so-called "Grays" or biomechanical androids that they used for abducting Terrans for their genetic programs. The most sinister of these could be described as a kind of false flag disinformation operation, one aimed at emulating the hybridization program being conducted by the avatars of the sea-based superorganism from the future. This cephalopod-type superorganism, aligned with the Prometheaion and with the assistance of some of the Ashuras, had been at work trying to engender or engineer (or perhaps conjure) a more evolved humanoid form of life. These childlike hybrids, who, with their large almond-shaped eyes and pointy chins, looked a lot like characters from Japanese anime, had an array of superhuman abilities. Despite their slight stature, their cognitive and psychic powers were such that they could be considered a deadly weapon in the struggle against the Olympians. So, the Olympians had taken it upon themselves to run their own hybridization program, with much more brutal abductions of sperm and egg donors and the repeated extraction of fetuses from female abductees. Instead of being superhumanly empowered and more evolved, the resulting hybrids were developmentally disabled. The Olympians intended to deny that they were running such a program at all and to blame it on "evil Grays," with the hybrids being construed as a demonic devolution of humanity.

Their end game was to target for persecutory extermination the actual hybrids, or changelings, who were being produced through a much more shamanic process. This is why they hid their genetic and embryological laboratories inside the Moon and managed to continue to do so for decades after their disclosure, in 2048, of the supposed "hybrid threat" and the putative violation of the personal sovereignty of abductees by the deviants that they portrayed as demonic enemies of the entire human community. Exposing these laboratories within the now naked space station was, consequently, a significant blow to this convoluted disinformation operation. It did not help that we also exposed these laboratories as the sites of human mutilations of the same type as the cattle mutilations, for which we revealed the Olympians to have been responsible as well — albeit using their android "Gray" minions to do this dirty work.

Most of the "lunar" structure was full of gigantic machinery devoted to a number of different purposes. Some of it was for maintenance of the station's structural integrity and the stability of its orbit. Other machinery was industrial in nature. But what was most disturbing to find, even more disturbing than the genetic laboratories, was the extensive psychotronic gadgetry that the Olympians had used from time immemorial to manipulate human souls, especially in the transition between death and rebirth. Following the missile strike and the identification of the shafts through which the Olympian saucers had entered and exited the Moon for millennia on their way to and back from Earth, we penetrated the interior of Artemis Station with a swarm of surveillance drones. These had enough time to document, among other things, the psychotronic machines and operations for the control of souls. (Gurdjieff had, albeit in a crude way, been more right than anyone would have believed. People *were* becoming "food for the Moon.")

All of this continued to be hidden even long after the Olympians revealed themselves in 2048 at the United Nations celebration for the centennial of the Universal Declaration of Human Rights held at the Palais de Chaillot in Paris. By that time, what was left of the scientific establishment had already abandoned materialism and mechanistic reductionism. That is not to say that the Spectral Revolution that I conceptualized had taken place, at least not in all of its dimensions and certainly not with its most profound consequences. That has taken until only the last few decades.

It is the year 2112. Or it would be, were we to have continued using the Gregorian or any other calendar relevant to that dead religion of Christianity. Now, time is measured in terms of the millennia that have elapsed since the destruction of Atlantis. That makes it the year 11676. Our struggle to defeat the Olympians, which oscillated in various epochs between a hot and a cold war, took nearly twelve thousand years to end in what could be considered a victory for Prometheans — albeit at tremendous cost. People call me Hyrcanius. Admiral Hyrcanius. It is a name that I chose after the past life regression that, like any other naturally (re)born member of our society, I underwent in my adolescence.

In my last lifetime — as Jorjani — I argued that the Spectral Revolution promised to be the greatest of all revolutions. The spectral, as in the phenomenon of light, is a spectrum that straddles the visible and the invisible (the ultra- and infra-frequencies). This spectrum underlies and underlines the artificiality of abstracting clearly defined qualities from out of the flux of experience, qualities that are often framed as binary oppositions, such as light and darkness, spiritual and material, hot and cold, male and female, truth and falsehood, reality and fiction, good and evil. The spectral is also what is yet to come or what haunts us from the future. As such, it signifies the flux of becoming that, over time, transforms seeming opposites into one another and reveals binaries and fixed categories as practical but transitory distinctions in the course of creative evolution. Last but not least, a specter is a ghost or spirit, and in this case the motivating spirit of technological science, namely Prometheus. This is the idea that technological development has a teleology driven by a kind of egregore or daimon, and that over time this specter reveals the technological essence of science. In other words, the "truth" is defined by what works (or can be made to work).

By the time the Olympians disclosed themselves in 2048, for well over a decade, every form of "psi" or psychic functioning—from extrasensory perception (ESP), such as Telepathy, Clairvoyance, and Precognition, to Psychokinesis (PK) at every scale—was being studied at world-class research institutions. But this kind of research, which had been done on the margins of establishment science for over a century at that point, however mainstream it then became, did not immediately yield any of the more profound psychological and sociological transformations indicated above—except for the revolutionary change in the conceptualization and *practice* of science. Even this took decades, since mainstream scientific recognition of psi was at first greeted with a flurry of frantic attempts to develop new all-encompassing theories that would accommodate these phenomena rather than to realize that their ultimate significance was to call for a post-paradigmatic science wherein theories are recognized as models with a pragmatic purpose.

To return to my point, this institutionalization of psi research also did little to prepare the public mind for processing the fact that what were conventionally understood to be human "souls" could be massively manipulated by a technology capable of interfacing with these "souls" considered as informational and energetic structures. Let alone that what we believed to be our Moon was honeycombed with this "psychotronic" technology, and that it was being used to keep the majority of the planet's population within a control system.

It was not until, in an act of desperation, our increasingly beleaguered rebel forces decided to attack the Moon in 2082 that we were able to reveal to some significant segment of the populace, who had hitherto accepted the Olympian overlords as saviors, that these "angels" or "devas" were actually psychotronic engineers hellbent on maintaining an archontic control over us at the most fundamental level. They had biomechanical devices with Artificial Intelligence, grown as much as manufactured, with quantum sensors and driven by quantum computers, which were capable of picking up the specific energetic frequency of the information processing matrices unique to one or another "soul" and then attracting these people into a controlled postmortem state.

The attractor appeared to the targeted individual as a white light leading into a tunnel, which acted as a soul magnet to draw that person into a number of possible constructs used to degrade their memory of the life that they had just lived and distract them from consciously and deliberatively determining the conditions of their own rebirth. In some cases, this would involve a heavenly vision wherein they would be welcomed by dead relatives and deities relevant to their belief system. In others, it would be a hellish experience. In many cases, this would follow a "life review" conducted by a panel of "guides" assumed to have divine authority. Then souls would be placed back into earthly life at a time that subjected them to certain astrological influences.

The robotic Grays played a key role in all this as spectral mechanics. Sometimes they would bungle things and carry off the wrong souls to the netherworld of the dead before the bookkeeping was corrected and the abductee was brought back with a terrifying tale about an NDE. An army of munchkins serving to perpetuate an illusionism of the kind that a Wizard of Oz could only hope to have at his disposal. In that analogy, the Wizard's control booth was the interior of the Moon and the men behind the curtain were the Olympians, who, by the time the curtain was pulled back, had gone a long way towards being accepted by the majority of Earth's demoralized population as the angels, gods, or divine ancestors of humanity. Being apprised of the nuts and bolts, as it were, of the lunar control booth for engineering the afterlife was, however, disillusioning to a large enough minority of these people to begin to tip the balance against Oz and in favor of our rebellion.

Once we managed, some years later, to actually shut down the psychotronic machines inside the now naked Moon, repurpose the Grays, and reappropriate the structure as Artemis Station, the end of interference in the transition between lifetimes made a significant impact on the mindset of even the most spiritually benighted Terrans. Astrological influence suddenly degraded. The Olympian Order that had seamlessly absorbed them as cells of a single social organism began to disintegrate and decohere.

Today the naked Moon, as viewed from Earth's surface or on approach from our colonies on Mars or in the asteroid belt, has become a symbol of revolutionary disclosure in general. I suppose that is fitting since, among the Amazons who first revered her, the name of Artemis — or *Arta-Amesha*, as they called her in their ancient Iranian tongue — meant "immortal Truth." The bow of the Huntress cannot but come to mind when Nietzsche, paraphrasing Herodotus, makes this the motto of his Zarathustra, "To speak the truth and shoot well with arrows, that is Persian virtue."

CHAPTER 2

ON PERSIAN VIRTUE

To say that the second quarter of the twenty-first century (of the old calendar system) was the age of inconvenient truths would be an understatement. Many convergent catastrophes, both engineered and apparently natural, shattered the modern world between 2025 and 2050. But it almost seemed as if these disasters were only the outward manifestation of far more profound inner calamities, experienced by individuals and societies grappling with the advent of unbearable truths. Poetic as this metaphor of psychical exteriorization may be, the fact is that the convergent catastrophes were the context for these devastating disclosures. Also accelerated by them as a means of manipulating the anticipated response with a view to catalyzing various deeply disempowering reactions on the part of the masses.

The first of these catastrophes was the Covid-19 pandemic and the mandatory mRNA vaccinations attendant to it. Engineered in a lab at Wuhan where the Chinese military also did bioweapons development, it was not the lab-leaked coronavirus itself that became the spearhead for the program of precipitous depopulation. Rather, the mRNA-based vaccines and booster shots developed by Western pharmaceutical companies — such as Pfizer, Moderna, and AstraZeneca — were the culprits. Throughout the Western world, including Australia, government agencies, such as the American FDA, knew that these vaccines had not undergone anything close to sufficient safety testing and trials before they mandated vaccination with them, including for children who could not give their consent and all military personnel.

As it turned out, within five years, these mRNA vaccines would cause the formation of bizarre white fibrous clots inside vital arteries. If this did not kill a person by causing cardiac arrest or a stroke, the spike protein synthesized by the genetically engineered vaccine would do serious neurological damage to some and catalyze the rapid growth of a variety of cancers in others. It began with athletes dying on sports fields. By 2025, the cases of mRNA-vaccinated people, especially those who had been young and healthy, who were just suddenly dropping dead, many of them on camera, became so ubiquitous that mainstream media attempts to suppress these stories were unsustainable.

It did not help that between 2022 and 2026, the birthrate in Western countries also collapsed to a level unseen since record-keeping started in the modern age. The sudden deaths and the stillbirths were all correlated to mRNA-vaccinated people, and autopsies of them inevitably revealed the artery-clotting long rubbery white fibers. Soon, there were more stillborn babies or miscarried fetuses than healthy children being born. Many other women simply couldn't get pregnant, and their menstrual cycles were very evidently affected.

The European NATO countries and Australia, led by the United States, were already a year into the Third World War before the dam of media suppression of this story broke in 2025. It helped that the adversaries of the North Atlantic Treaty Organization wanted the story out, since neither China nor Russia had used mRNA technology to develop their much safer Covid vaccines. By the time American and allied NATO forces were at war with Russia in Eastern Europe and had engaged China in and around Taiwan, the majority of these soldiers were already dying of strokes, heart attacks, a variety of cancers, or they were debilitated by thyroid dysfunction, multiple sclerosis, cognitive impairment, severe insomnia, immune dysfunction, blood clots, avascular necrosis, and liver dysfunction. The militaries of the

Western countries, Australia included in the Pacific theater, literally collapsed in the face of their Eastern foes.

That was abroad. At home, America and Western Europe were devastated by the Chinese and Russian use of unconventional weapons that were capable of mimicking natural catastrophes. These included both weather weapons and tectonic weaponry. The East Coast of the United States was hit by engineered hurricanes of unprecedented ferocity, as well as floods, droughts, and forest fires. Meanwhile, a European Union already starved for energy resources—including for winter heating—was pummeled by snowstorms and cold spells that froze millions of already sick people to death. Tectonic weapons were used to trigger massive earthquakes both at Cumbre Vieja, resulting in a flank collapse on Las Palmas, and at the Cascadia subduction zone. The tsunamis from both earthquakes cost millions of Americans their lives. The one in the Atlantic drowned New York City. The one in the Pacific flooded Vancouver, Seattle, and Portland.

Then came the death blow to the West, or the "kill shot," as it was called by some. From the perspective of Easterners, who had long resented the West, it appeared to be God's Justice or the Mandate of Heaven. In 2025, a solar magnetic storm of at least equal magnitude to the Carrington Event scorched the Western hemisphere of the Earth with coronal mass ejections. In an area extending from Western Europe through the Americas, the electromagnetic pulses (EMP) of the solar flares essentially destroyed the power grid, cut the phone lines, and rendered electronic devices useless. Airplanes fell out of the sky onto crowded cities and empty fields. Cars were stopped dead on the road, and trains with equally fried electronic circuitry screeched to a halt on their tracks.

What was already a supply chain crisis turned into a total collapse of goods shipments. Even diesel-based trucks could not navigate highways that were littered with burned-out cars. Commuters cut off from their workplaces meant that what little was by that point left of urban and suburban America really came apart at the seams. Western

Europe fared somewhat better, but the devastation of the solar storm, when combined with the exploded time bomb of the mRNA vaccine, resulted in a situation wherein Russian forces were able to roll across the continent relatively unopposed, all the way to the French border with Germany.

France had managed to avert occupation by making a separate peace with Russia and China in the Spring of 2027, when its new right-wing government withdrew France from NATO rather than using the French nuclear arsenal as an umbrella for the defense of Europe in a war that America had started. This was one of the key developments that turned the United Nations into a world government by 2028.

The other was the Second American Civil War. The fact that this conflict took place simultaneously with the Third World War was obviously a significant factor in the total defeat of NATO, an organization that everyone understood to be the American Empire in everything but name. The Second Civil War started in the aftermath of the 2024 US Presidential Election, so by the time the frying of the power grid cut effective communication and transportation across the vast expanse of the continental United States, regional divides had already prepared the ground for America's disintegration. Actually, it did not stop at the borders of the Former USA and extended into Canada. Six new nations came into being: the Republic of Cascadia (British Columbia, Washington State, and Oregon), the California Republic, the Confederate States of America, the Republic of Quebec, Gotham (New York and New Jersey), and the Commonwealth of New England. Next to these was a much smaller United States of America (with its capital in Colorado) and what was left of Canada.

With the exception of the new Confederacy, all of the newly "independent" nations remained in the United Nations as it was restructured into a world government. Quebec had wavered and considered an alliance with the Confederacy, but Quebec did not want to fall out with France, which played such a key role in reforming the UN and insisted that China and Russia use this institution to advance their hegemony somewhat more legitimately.

The most significant consequence of the collapse of the USA was the de facto declassification of devastating secrets long held in the vaults of the CIA, the NSA, and the Pentagon. It was not so much declassification or disclosure as it was the fact that once the federal government ceased to function across most of the former states of the Union, high-ranking military and intelligence officials who found themselves citizens of the new nations of North America were effectively released from their national security and secrecy oaths. Certain of the new republics in particular considered testimony from these officials to be an important part of starting with a clean slate, and they offered amnesty or immunity from prosecution to those who made these confessions. Once they became the undisputed victors of the Third World War, China and Russia also exerted significant pressure, through the UN, to make sure that these Truth Tribunals took place. The truth about the Covid-19 vaccine as a genocidally depopulating bioweapon had already dynamited the stigma of "conspiracy theories" that the mainstream media in America had used to keep these terrible truths hidden for decades.

The two most significant disclosures were closely connected to one another insofar as they exposed a single cabal that, since at least the 1950s, had succeeded in capturing the most fundamental levels of strategic planning and policymaking in the USA. It was a military-industrial-intelligence-corporate structure, which President Eisenhower had tried to warn the American people about on his way out of office in 1960. He had also tried to privately, and more substantively, warn incoming President Kennedy. But alas, when JFK attempted to act on Ike's warning, threatening to break up the CIA and to collaborate with the Soviet Union on the frontier of the Moon, this cabal orchestrated his public execution at Dealey Plaza in Dallas. The same people were responsible for the assassinations of the patsy Lee Harvey Oswald, Robert Kennedy, Marilyn Monroe, Martin Luther King, and at least half a dozen other people of lesser notoriety who were connected to them.

A generation later, this cabal orchestrated the controlled demolition of the Twin Towers in Manhattan and a missile strike on the Pentagon in Washington on September 11, 2001. What some of the former insiders revealed to Americans about the "inside job" on 9/11 was even more outrageous than what they had to come to terms with regarding the Kennedy Assassination. The deliberate incineration of nearly three thousand American citizens by people holding positions of power in the state security services of their own government was so appalling a truth to fathom that all nuance was lost on those who were being asked to grapple with it. International connections, such as to Deutsche Bank, were rendered irrelevant by comparison to how many US officials in sensitive positions were implicated in the vast conspiracy to commit mass murder and justify two illegal wars, in Afghanistan and Iraq, both of which actually served to strengthen the Islamists who were blamed for the supposed acts of "terrorism." Well, it *was* terrorism. But the terrorists were in the CIA, the NSA, the Department of Defense, and even within the Bush-Cheney cabinet itself. No one traced the web woven by these men back to the Spider of the Fourth Reich, which had actually infiltrated the US Government and masterminded the attacks in an attempt to lay the groundwork for the eventual destruction of liberal-democratic America. The trust in mainstream media was so shattered by these disclosures that, by 2030, almost no one believed *anything* that was reported over "the news." Belief, in any subject, became strictly a matter of faith, and secularism, with its commitment to objective truths, collapsed in the face of a rabid and, in many cases, violent resurgence of religious sectarianism and rival political cults.

Europe had its own version of the disclosure of truths that were not just inconvenient but were for many unbearable. A number of European nations followed France out of NATO in 2027, but these did not align themselves with France and they also left the beleaguered

European Union. Nor were they eager to join a reformed United Nations that was becoming no more than an instrument for the legitimization of the new Chinese and Russian hegemony, welcomed by the other BRICS nations that were stakeholders in the new order. On account of their cessation of hostilities with Russia, these Central and Eastern European countries were able to avoid the Russian occupation that hardcore dead-ender NATO states such as Germany were initially subjected to.

Foremost among them was Italy, which expelled US forces from its territory in late 2027. The rest were Central, Eastern, and Southeastern European nations, most of which had, before the war, attempted to combine their efforts by forming the Visegrád Group. Poland, the former de facto leader of this group, suffered Russian occupation, having remained faithful to NATO until the war's end, and having then served as the corridor for Russia's invasion of Germany. Instead, the group was now effectively led by Italy. Other notable members were Greece, Austria, Hungary, and Romania. The coalition was Fascist. There are no two ways about it, unless one wants to claim that it was too Traditionalist to even be considered properly Fascist. From the perspective of the Russians, who considered their new Eurasian Order to be an embodiment of what Alexander Dugin called "the Fourth Political Theory," this Central Eastern European bloc represented a resurgence of "the Third Political Theory." In any case, the racist — or, as they liked to put it, "racialist" — and reactionary politics of this bloc was legitimated by the reframing of certain taboo subjects as truths long suppressed by the Anglo-American Empire.

The first of these served to justify the forcible expulsion of all those African and Middle Eastern migrants who had flooded into these parts of Europe in the early twenty-first century as a consequence of American interventions that produced failed states in Islamic countries, such as Libya and Syria. That was a truth having to do with the genetic basis not only of IQ but of human achievement in general. Statistically rigorous empirical studies of this subject, long marginalized to the fringes of the scientific establishment, began to appear in respectable publications connected to leading research institutions and universities in the reactionary parts of Europe.

As for other universities that pushed back against these studies, those in Western Europe and liberal parts of America in particular, these had lost almost all of their credibility. No one who wanted a real education attended these institutions, and it was understood that most of the history and science that they taught, at least since the middle of the twentieth century, had been false. Their geology, archeology, and anthropology were widely perceived to have been equally false. In some cases, such as Physics, a conspiracy to suppress entire alternate paradigms was now recognized to have been in place since the late nineteenth century. The same loss of trust was true of primary and preparatory public schools in the West. By 2040, they were mostly replaced with homeschooling. But I am getting sidetracked. My point was that these genetic studies appeared to demonstrate, beyond statistical doubt, that IQ and other factors linked to human achievement in industry, science, and the arts varied greatly based on the genetic heritage of ethnically distinct populations.

As far as IQ was concerned, ethnic Europeans (including in the Americas) were in the highest bracket, together with two other groups: the Han Chinese and Ashkenazi Jews. Other genetically clustered populations, such as Arabs and especially Africans, fell far below them, and this was reflected in every achievement having to do with mathematical and spatial reasoning. The greatness of the Islamic World in science and technology during the period of 900–1100 in the old Gregorian calendar had to do with the fact that 90% of these so-called "Islamic" scientists and inventors were actually Persians and other Iranians who at that time still retained their "Aryan" genes and had yet to be sufficiently miscegenated by admixture with Arabs, Turks, and Mongols. Once this miscegenation and the genocide of the directive elite of Iran (*Aryana*) by these successive waves of non-Aryan invaders took place, scientific and technological achievement in Iran collapsed (until the mid-twenty-first century, but we will come to that shortly).

However, IQ, or the measure of mathematical and spatial reasoning, was only one criterion of the aptitude for human achievement. Whereas the Han Chinese were together with Europeans (and, in the past, some Indo-Europeans, such as the Iranians) in the highest bracket of IQ, on the level of population genetics they lacked the complex factors that accounted for the Western (and ancient Persian and Scythian) proclivity toward innovation, exploration, experimentation, and every form of bold creativity, risk-taking, and novelty-seeking. According to the many studies that were being published in European scientific journals in the 2030s, these population traits were also genetic in basis, and they were to account for the evident Western supremacy in all of the arts, from literature and painting to architecture, music, and cinema.

The Jews, the Ashkenazim to be specific, were a special case. Unlike the original Semitic Jews (who remained genetically very close to Arabs), the Ashkenazim were a hybrid population of Indo-Europeans from the Western coastal territories of the Caspian Sea, in the Caucasus, who had been miscegenated by incoming Turks. Their Khazar Kingdom had adopted Judaism for political reasons, to help shore up its independence from both Christendom and the Caliphate. Despite sharing with Europeans both high IQ and also a significant aptitude for creative achievement and the kind of exploratory curiosity that leads to innovation, these Ashkenazim, who constituted most of European Jewry, were once again stigmatized by the reactionary forces of Traditionalist Europe.

This is where the first of the unbearable truths that became institutionalized in parts of Europe converged with the second one, a subject that had been at least equally taboo in the years before World War III. It was, in fact, a subject inextricable from World War II, and its reevaluation only took place when the history of that war, which. like all history that is written by the victors, was overwritten by the vicissitudes of another World War.

I am talking about "the Holocaust" of European Jews. The word "holocaust" technically means to destroy by means of fire. The oldest record of it that we have is actually the holocaust committed by the Jews against the native population of Canaan, for example at Jericho, where Yahweh ordered his chosen people to burn everyone and everything in the city, including the animals, and to salvage only the gold and other valuables that could be looted. That European Jews were themselves subjected to a burning by fire was not called into question by scholars and statesmen of the reactionary bloc in Europe. But that they were burned with anything like the same genocidal intentionality that ancient Israel was founded upon is what was denied by these reactionaries on the basis of what had been hidden data.

Much of this data supposedly came from out of the breached archives of British Intelligence after the total collapse of the United Kingdom in the last years of the Third World War. Certain MI6 defectors with right-wing sympathies, who made their way to Austria and Italy at the end of the war, helped to "bring this information to light" and "to expose" (as they put it) the manner in which the British, with approval from their OSS American allies, had manufactured the narrative of "the Holocaust" toward the end of World War II. The revised narrative regarding "the Holocaust," which became entrenched in the reactionary parts of Europe and was well-received by many in the BRICS countries as it became widely disseminated across a new post-Western international media, was as follows. Whether it is accurate or not, I cannot say. Only that a new constellation of power established it as "the truth" and, moreover, a "truth" with the aura of something so long suppressed as a catastrophic danger to society that its putative "disclosure" was lent the weight of Revelation.

It was claimed that, to begin with, Jews were only one among a number of minority and dissident groups that were sent to forced labor camps once the Allied Powers declared war on Germany after limited and legitimate German territorial annexations. These minorities and dissidents included Gypsies and even Christian Gentile Germans, such as rogue priests who had protested against the National Socialist regime. In other words, the rationale for their being sentenced to forced labor was that they could not be relied upon as patriotic citizens in a time of war, nor could they be trusted to serve in the armed forces. The Gypsies were put in that category because of their transnational trafficking activities. The Jews of Germany were in it because they were a part of international Jewry that had organized an international boycott of German goods beginning in 1933 when Hitler came to power. After this boycott, the Jewish "traitors" were asked to leave Germany. Once World War II began in 1939, those who did not leave started to be sent to forced labor camps. That is what Auschwitz, Belzec, Treblinka, and so forth were. The motto above the camp gates, "Work makes you free," essentially meant "prove your loyalty to the state."

These were concentration camps of the very same kind that the British invented and used in South Africa in the early twentieth century. They only became "death camps" when the British Royal Air Force bombed the train lines supplying these labor camps with food and medicine. Starvation and disease broke out in the camps, as was the intention of the British war planners. Together with the other inmates, including the dissident Gentile Germans, the Jews began to starve to death and succumb to highly infectious diseases spread by lice, such as typhus.

Zyklon B was a delousing agent. Its purpose was to kill lice to prevent the spread of disease. The "gas chambers" at these camps were designed for that purpose, namely, to delouse workers for contagion containment. Not to kill anyone. The Jews *and other forced laborers* in the camps were not "gassed to death." They died of starvation and disease, and because their starved bodies were diseased and highly infectious, the cadavers had to be burned for the sake of sterilization.

The industrial ovens that were frantically repurposed for this by SS officers were never intended to be used to "holocaust" anyone. Moreover, the number of people whose already starved and diseased cadavers were disposed of by this horrible means of improvised sterilization was, according to the now institutionalized reactionaries of Europe, a number far lower than the supposed "6 million" figure invented by British Intelligence in collaboration with Zionists (based on the Cabalistic significance of this number). Rather, they claimed it was more like 2.5 million. Again, this included many non-Jews. The number was supposedly inflated in part with a view to minimizing the horrendous scale of the war crimes committed by the Allied Powers against hundreds of thousands of civilians who were deliberately incinerated in Dresden, Tokyo, Hiroshima, and Nagasaki.

Unfortunately, denial of the mantra of "the Holocaust of Six Million Jews" had become tantamount to apostasy in the pre-Third World War era, such that as much as it had been impossible to have a rational and empirical discussion of the subject in those days, the reaction to the revised facts was equally irrational and impassioned. First of all, few people went to the trouble to check these supposedly new "facts." Secondly, hardly anyone was concerned to point out that the Jews, as much as the other minorities and dissidents who were victimized, had no business being in those forced labor camps to begin with. Or, for that matter, even being deported and packed into trains like chattel under the most appalling conditions. It was lost on most enraged Europeans that so many blameless — and in some cases brilliant — individuals ought not to have suffered and perished in such an appalling manner for the putative "disloyalty" of some amorphous group ("The Jews") with which a lot of them did not identify whatsoever. Many of "the Jews" who wound up at these camps considered themselves part of the cultural community of the country that they came from and did not practice Judaism or have anything tangible in common with other "Jews."

It was certain Nietzschean-minded Zionists who wanted to use trauma to bind together under this ancient brand these poor secular individuals accustomed to metropolitan European life, so as to convince them that their only refuge was a god-forsaken piece of desert in the Middle East. The leadership of these Zionists had been secretly collaborating with the Nazis with a view to the "final solution" of the establishment of the State of Israel, to the extent that coins were even minted in Nazi Germany between 1938 and 1940 with the Swastika on one side and the Star of David on the other. The Nazi plan for Palestine, which they wanted to seize from the British colonizers of that land, was to turn it into a new state for European Jews, modeled on National Socialism or Fascism, allied with Nazi Germany, and constructed in collaboration with German Zionists.

The Russians still prided themselves on having been the principal force to defeat the Nazis in World War II, but the Russians were, to say the least, unpopular in reactionary Europe, and World War III had ended with the total destruction of the Anglo-American Establishment. (France, with its connection to Quebec and to certain American rogues, was all that was left of Atlanticism.) In the 2030s, precisely a century after its rise, German National Socialism and even the personage of Adolf Hitler himself were reevaluated from his native Austria to Italy, which had, after all, been Nazi Germany's closest ally. Mussolini was also reframed as a national hero by a majority of Italians.

What all of this meant was that as it approached what should have been its centennial celebration (in 2048), the State of Israel was almost completely abandoned, isolated, and defeated. First of all, as one of the most aggressive states in enforcing mandatory mRNA vaccination across its population, by the end of the Third World War in 2028, the Israelis were decimated by the same degenerative and ultimately lethal effects of the mRNA vaccines and booster shots. Even their once impressive military was in shambles, and their only remaining defense was their nuclear arsenal and the few personnel that they had left who were capable of delivering those nukes by means of fighter jets and submarines. But geopolitically and economically, Israel would have been totally destroyed but for a new and unexpected ally — well, only unexpected to those ignorant of the long arc of history. Iran.

When the rest of the world turned its back on Israel and when contempt for the Jews reached a new zenith surpassing that of the 1930s, the Persian griffin of post-Islamic Iran took Israel and the Jewish diaspora under her wings. Israel, in turn, joined Iran, and thereby also joined forces with Prometheism, to become a new David standing against the goliath of an emerging Chinese global hegemony wrapped in the flag of the United Nations.

This was surprising only to those unaware of the tremendous role that ancient Iran played in the reestablishment of Israel after the Babylonian exile. Not only was Cyrus the Great the sole gentile to ever be hailed as a "Messiah" by the Jews for freeing them from Babylon, but the rebuilding of the Temple of Solomon at Jerusalem, namely the Second Temple Project, which Cyrus commissioned at a cost to the Persian treasury was actually executed and completed by his successor, Darius the Great. Darius also laid the groundwork of the international banking and credit system, working in cooperation with the Jews of Babylon — a city that had become the administrative capital of Imperial Iran. Then there was the third great Shah of Achaemenid Iran, Xerxes, who, while waging a relentless war on Greece, also acted to save the Jews of his empire from being liquidated by a treacherous Prime Minister, albeit with the help of his Jewish Queen, Esther, and her uncle, Mordechai, who Xerxes made his new Vizier. That Iran would reclaim her historical relationship with the Jews together with the other glories of her pre-Islamic heritage made perfect sense, especially considering the reentry of so many wealthy and influential Persian Jews into Iran after the fall of the Islamic Republic.

That would have been true even if it were not for the fact that most Iranians came to see Israel as their liberator, in a kind of historical repayment of the debt owed to the children of Cyrus. The third major front of the Third World War was opened in the Middle East by Israel, which launched extensive air strikes on the Iranian nuclear facilities in 2025. This came on the heels of a total loss of legitimacy of the Islamic Republic in the Western world after the regime chose to dig its heels in by using the Islamic Revolutionary Guard Corps (IRGC) and their Basij militia of millions of zealous Shiites to massacre protesters who had brought the theocratic government to the brink of collapse after a year and a half of nationwide demonstrations and general strikes. Sadly, it was not the Iranian National Military who, in a much hoped-for coup, stepped up to save citizens from the IRGC. That nationalist coup never materialized. Instead, it was Israel.

Once the IRGC retaliated against the Israeli air strikes by bombarding Israel with ballistic missiles launched from Iran, some of them with chemical warheads, as well as drone strikes fielded from out of Hezbollah strongholds in Lebanon and Syria, Israel launched a full-spectrum attack — using both its fighter jets and submarines — on every IRGC target inside of Iran and in the waters of the Persian Gulf. It is only once the IRGC was destroyed, by Israel, together with other key regime targets, such as the Office of the Supreme Leader, the Parliament, and the Judiciary, that demonstrators and their opposition leadership were able to definitively overthrow the Islamic Republic.

As already noted above, Israel would go on to collapse in the face of the consequences of its mRNA vaccine mandates, but by the time that happened, the Israelis had regained their ancient Iranian ally. For its part, Iran was entirely unscathed by the vaccine catastrophe, since one thing that could be said for the Islamic Republic is that it had banned the use of mRNA vaccines in Iran. (The Iranians had developed their own Covid vaccine, similar to that of the Chinese and Russians.)

Those Iranians who overthrew the Islamic Republic had been expecting to find themselves embraced and their country reconstructed by the Western world. But the West collapsed in the very same years that the new secular democratic regime of Iran emerged. Iranians had come to hate China and Russia, who had backed the repression of the

Islamic Republic for so long, and who were leading the new order, albeit with France insisting that this post-Western system nominally take shape under the flag of the United Nations. France, for its part, had been significantly devastated by both the vaccine and the war, and was in no position to offer significant assistance to the new Iran. Rhetorically, there was a renewed Franco-Iranian friendship, but this was only lukewarm on account of the degree of French deference to Russia, the Islamic Republic's last and most ardent ally. So, Israel, which found itself devastated, isolated, and more broadly opposed than ever, entered into a profound partnership with a new Iran that the Israeli destruction of the IRGC helped bring into being.

Looking back on my last life as Jorjani, I am proud to have played a key role in brokering that partnership as part of Operation Hyrcanian Storm or the project of building a Promethean Persia. By the time our Promethean Pirates had built their first two seasteads, between the Tunb Islands and Abu Musa in the Persian Gulf and in the south Caspian Sea off the coast of Hyrcania, we were acting as the single most powerful conduit for Iranian-Israeli cooperation, especially in domains that had to remain clandestine. For example, under the Traditionalist and regressive mindset of the de facto world government that the Chinese and Russians had, with the acquiescence of the French, turned the United Nations into, genetic engineering of humans was prohibited by law. The UN intended to punish even the numerous nations that had left the organization for violating any of its laws, but this was largely not a problem for them in the area of advanced technologies, such as gene editing, because most of those countries that left the UN as it became a world government were even more Traditionalist than the new Sino-Russian leadership of the UN — for example, Confederate America or the reactionary Europa Group. But the Iranians and Israelis were both very interested in genetic engineering. The Israelis were hoping to use it to reverse the damage of the mRNA vaccination. The Iranians to eugenically enhance their population.

Our Promethean resistance to the Chinese-dominated World State was largely fueled, in its early years, by its piratical facilitation of classified joint Iranian-Israeli research and development in the domain of a variety of prohibited Singularity-level technologies. How ironic that, after bombing the Iranian nuclear facilities to smithereens, the Israelis cooperated in the reconstruction of Iran's nuclear weapons capability, albeit under the cover of the flaming black flag of Prometheism and its pirate navy. They were Iran's nukes in the sense that we had negotiated joint custody of them with black ops personnel in Iranian military intelligence. This was to ensure that they would be used for, among other purposes, deterrence of any threat to Iran's territorial integrity and the defense of Iran's relative independence from the coercive and regressive globalism of the UN. By 2040, Promethean Persia was a secret nuclear power.

Frankly, these nukes were peanuts — or rather, pistachios — compared to some of the developments that both overt and covert Iranian-Israeli collaboration yielded. In 2045, two decades after the fall of the Islamic Republic, Zero Point Energy (ZPE) technology was at the disposal of Iran for both energy production and space propulsion. In a debt of gratitude to the Israeli and 'Jewish' (they were secular) diaspora scientists who helped make this possible, Iranian space missions included Israeli astronauts together with Iranian ones. Of course, these were not strictly "national" or bilateral space missions. They were cosmopolitan or *cosmopiratical* Promethean endeavors, but Iranians and Israelis were overrepresented per the size of their populations as compared to the many other countries from which Promethean individuals participating in these intrepid expeditions hailed. The position of a new Iran, as both a benefactor and beneficiary of Prometheism, in the second quarter of the twenty-first century (of the old calendar) was at the nexus of two of the philosophical concepts that I developed in my life as Jorjani.

The first of these is the World State of Emergency. That means a State of Emergency of global scope, as well as the emergence of a

World State from this planet-wide crisis. Carl Schmitt argued that the nature of sovereign authority is revealed amidst a State of Emergency when the constitutional law is suspended and government cannot function in a normal representative or legislative manner. Generally, such crises reveal features of sovereign power that, in principle, seem as if they could never be globalized, such as the fact that the sovereign can maintain order without law because he embodies the ethos of his people, and the fact that the sovereign decides on the distinction between the friends and enemies of a state. If there is no global ethos and if humanity as a whole cannot have an external enemy (since the enemy of one or another community does not cease to be human), then one might assume that there cannot be a global sovereign. However, in *World State of Emergency* (2017), I argued that this changes with the convergent advancement of technologies that question the very boundary conditions of humanity itself. Singularity-level technologies confront humanity as a whole with a potentially inhuman existential threat, including from a combat theater in intra-lunar space that defines the entire Earth as a geopolitical entity in need of sovereign order.

The World State that ultimately emerged from out of these pressures was a more cohesive and coercive form of the United Nations, which relocated its headquarters to the Palais des Nations in Geneva in 2028 and was dominated by Confucian China, Orthodox Russia, and Traditionalist Islam. These paternalistic Traditionalists also adopted certain aspects of the Luddite "back to nature" discourse of Deep Ecology. Under their leadership, the UN wound up being driven by a reactionary and regressive attempt to cut off and roll back humanity's approach toward both the Technological Singularity and the Spectral Revolution, seeing these inextricable developments as "Satanic" sins of Promethean pride. It makes perfect sense that, after the collapse of the West, Iran would wind up becoming the spearhead of this "Satanic" Counter-Traditionalism. Not Iran as a nation, but Iran as the most densely vibrant concentration of intensity in a global blockchain-based Promethean Network State with a crypto economy rivaling the regulated economy of the UN.

This has to do with the dialectical forces that, over the course of twenty-five centuries of Iran's recorded history, determined the dynamics of how the new Iran took shape after the revolutionary overthrow of the Islamic Republic. Early on, most historians analyzing the Iranian Revolution of 2022–2025 were limited to considering sociological and political forces that had been in play, from the Persian Constitutional Revolution of 1905–1911, which, but for British and Russian meddling, would have produced the first parliamentary democracy in the Middle East, through to Prime Minister Mossadegh's bid for Iran's freedom and independence from 1951–1953, and of course the 1979 Islamic Revolution that brought into being the regime overthrown in 2025 after 46 years of theocratic tyranny. But when viewed against the far more expansive horizon of Iranian history since the time of Zarathustra and the Achaemenids, one could say with a griffin's eye view, much deeper dialectical forces came into sight as they worked themselves out in the collective unconscious of the Iranians to yield the Promethean Persia of the mid-twenty-first century. These forces had to do with the struggle for freedom and progress, two ideas or ideals that were at the core of Zarathustra's gospel.

I owe my concept of Being Bound for Freedom to this ancient Iranian wellspring. Being Bound for Freedom means how Being or Existence has to be structured in order for there to be free will, namely without an all-knowing or an almighty God and also without any deterministic laws of Nature. It also means that Being is headed towards ever greater freedom, in the sense of the history of revolutions and liberation struggles, beginning with the rebellion of Prometheus against Olympus on behalf of mankind. Finally, it means the willingness to be bound, like Prometheus, as a punishment for being a freedom fighter against one or another form of tyranny, and this is also a binding in the sense of a conscientious duty. All three meanings are clearly connected because it is the nature of existence that is revealing itself over time in the destruction of various forms of oppression, and martyrs are revealed amidst such revolutions.

This concept, which I explicated in several of the books that I wrote in my past life as Jorjani, is clearly extrapolated from out of the Iranian conceptions of *Âzâdegi* and *Spentâ Mainyu* — in other words, "free-spiritedness" (of which free will is an indispensable precondition) and the "progressive mentality" that is the single most defining quality of *Ahurâ Mazdâ*, the "titan of Wisdom," who is a more abstract and less anthropomorphic form of the ancient Caucasian deity who becomes "Prometheus" for the Greeks. *Promethea* or "forward-thinking" is an almost literal Greek cognate of *Spentâ Mainyu,* and the creative force of *Ahurâ Mazdâ,* whose divine intellect is epitomized by this quality, has, from the time of Zarathustra onward, been symbolized by the eternal fire. The fire of the torch of liberty, the firestorm of revolutions and their transmutation of societies reaching for that final transformation of the world that Zarathustra called the *Frashgard.*

Long before the modern revolutions of Iran, the Mazdakite Revolution of 488–531 could be identified as not only the most radical revolution of the whole world prior to the modern age, but perhaps the most pivotal event in Iran's entire history. Historical records indicate that the movement that came to power in that revolution and seized the government of Iran for an entire generation under the nominal authority of Kavad I was already more than two hundred years old at the time, having been the principal force of resistance against the institutionalization of Orthodox Zoroastrianism by Ardeshir Babakan when he founded the Sassanian dynasty in 212.

Then, following the reactionary counter-revolution of Khosrow I in 531, in the course of which Mazdak and a hundred thousand of his followers were put to death in order to restore Orthodoxy, the Mazdakite movement went underground and survived for another three hundred years until Babak Khorramdin took up its mantle in the 830s, when it was rebranded as the Khorramdin or Khorrami movement, the single most powerful Iranian rebellion against the

Arab-Muslim Caliphate based in Baghdad. With "liberty or death" being his motto, scaled to today's population, in his struggle to free Iran, Babak killed millions of his fellow Iranians who were collaborating with the Caliphate or acquiescing to Arab-Muslim domination and life under Islamic law.

What happened in Iran from 2030–2040 cannot be understood without the Mazdakite revolutionary movement and its Khorramite resurgence being considered a profound historical precedent. What these people were fighting for — from the 220s to the 830s! — was not only freedom but the most progressive interpretation of Zarathustra's gospel of progress, and what they stood against was, in the first instance, a conservative theocratic perversion of Zarathustra by the Orthodox Zoroastrianism of the Sassanid state, and, in the second case, the totalitarian repression of Islam and its Sharia law.

Orthodox Zoroastrians had either fled to India, where they became the "Parsis" (Persians) of Bombay, or they were *dehghans* (aristocratic lords) who cut deals with the Arab Caliphs to preserve their feudal landholdings in Iran. It was the Mazdakite revolutionary movement that reemerged to do the most damage to the Caliphate. Had the Mazdakite movement not been so brutally repressed by the Sassanids, which effectively shattered the Iranian state by angering the Parthian Lords and Ladies who still adhered to heterodox Mithraism, and had backed Mazdak against the central government, Iran would probably never have fallen to the Arab invasion of 651. Iran fell because the Mithraic Parthian Houses who had backed the Mazdakite revolution from above refused to fight for the Sassanids, and a significant segment of the population who had been the backbone of that revolution from beneath was so disgusted by the House of Sassan that they wanted to see the central government in Ctesiphon fall. They did not expect that the Arabs would succeed in carrying the banner of Islam east of the Zagros Mountains.

In any case, the flourishing of science, technology, and the arts in Iran from 900–1100 had to do with the relative success of the

Khorrami movement and other related and allied revolts against the Arabian Caliphate by Neo-Mithraic leaders of Parthian origin from Greater Hyrcania, such as Afshin, Mazyar, Sunpadh (Sinbad) and Ishaq. It is they who weakened the Baghdad Caliphs to the point where the Buyid and Samanid dynasties in Rayy (Tehran), Samarkand, and Bukhara could become patrons of the Iranian Renaissance in the epoch of Razi, Khwarizmi, and Ferdowsi.

Centuries-long dialectical forces like these are recorded in, as it were, the "Akashic record" of a country's collective unconscious. Those who mistook the Iranian Revolution of 2022–2025 as the culmination of the Persian Constitutional Revolution's aim of establishing a system wherein "the rule of law" would be paramount were blind to these deeper forces that bound Iran for a freedom beyond any legalistic legitimacy of the kind that the United Nations came to monopolize. The teleological forward momentum of freedom for the sake of progress, which had defined the long arc of Iranian history from Zarathustra and the Achaemenids onward, would not bend before any regressive UN regulations in the name of "sustainable development" post-2030.

Instead, Persia would become the bastion of Promethean rebellion against the World State, just as the Parthians had backed and benefited from their intimate relationship with the Cilician pirates who first flew the black flag in the waters of the Mediterranean and who played the largest role in spreading the fire of Mithraism into Roman society through the Empire's ports. Our blazing black banner is a successor to theirs, and we Promethean pirates became their legitimate heirs.

CHAPTER 3

THE OLYMPIAN ORDER

IRAN IS ONE of the most high-altitude nations in the world, with 70% of the country consisting of three tall mountain ranges. The fact that we were able to base ourselves here as well as in the oceans, including underwater, meant that we were fairly well prepared to secure an asymmetrical advantage in the wake of the catastrophe that took place in 2039, right after Iran left the United Nations. The Earth's magnetic field had been weakening for decades, and there had been signs of the migration of the magnetic poles. In late 2039, just as the world was taking the first step toward recovery from the preceding convergent catastrophes, the magnetic poles of the Earth shifted. Attendant electrical and tectonic activity loosened the crust from the mantle, setting off volcanoes all over the planet as the crust slipped for thousands of kilometers, causing the geographical poles to shift as well. The oceans were tossed out of their basins onto coastal areas in tsunamis that destroyed what cities were left functioning on the Pacific Rim. Among the consequences of this pole shift was that Antarctica got pulled out from the southern polar region.

Queen Maud Land and other coastal regions of Antarctica had already begun to melt when, in 2042, an undetected asteroid approaching from the direction of the Sun, and masked by its glare, broke into a few fragments as it entered Earth's atmosphere. The largest chunk of it smashed into the Antarctic ice sheet. The glacier was shattered into ice cubes around the Transantarctic Mountains. Then the continent began to thaw much faster, precipitously raising the global sea level. The skyscrapers of Manhattan went under water up to the thirtieth floor of the Empire State Building. At the same time, the hitherto occulted titanic architecture and engineering of Atlantis reemerged relatively intact — having been well preserved by the ice over the course of nearly 11,700 years. The time had come for the Olympians, who had destroyed that world, to reveal and explain themselves.

Let me paint a picture of the world situation when these Olympians publicly addressed the planet in December of 2048 during the centennial celebration of the signing of the Universal Declaration of Human Rights at the Palais de Chaillot in Paris. Although, as I mentioned earlier, by this time the headquarters of the United Nations had been moved from New York, which was flooded, to the Palais des Nations in Geneva, which had been the seat of the old League of Nations, it was the Musée de l'Homme on the Trocadéro in Paris that was chosen for the address.

A fitting choice since this anthropological museum was dedicated to the evolutionary prehistory and historical development of mankind. This was why, after having been established in 1937, the Palais de Chaillot, within which the museum is located, was chosen as the site for the signing of the Universal Declaration of Human Rights (UDHR) by the delegates of the UN General Assembly in 1948 (before the General Assembly became based at the headquarters constructed for that purpose in New York). The museum contained everything from prehistoric Venus sculptures to the skull of René Descartes. Claude Lévi-Strauss had once been the director. What could have been more perfect as a venue for "gods" who wanted to present themselves as the hitherto occulted Ancestors and Guardians of humanity?

The single gleaming saucer landed right on the square-inlaid stone pattern of the Trocadéro terrace, across from the Eiffel Tower and between the Palais de Chaillot and the Musée national de la Marine de Paris. The latter was a maritime artifacts and artworks museum, which was also apropos since these saucers were trans-medium vehicles and these Nordics were more rightly regarded as stealthy denizens of our own ocean depths than they were space travelers. Their representative stepped out of the saucer before the cameras of the assembled media, who had also been live broadcasting the discus on its descent. (A no-fly zone had been put into place over the area by the United Nations Air Force.) Then, with one look across at the Eiffel Tower, he strode quickly but confidently into the Palais de Chaillot together with his escort of dark-suited dignitaries and armed security personnel.

Later he would be given a televised tour of both museums flanking his parked saucer, which made for memorable images of this platinum-haired, paternally angelic figure overlooking the anthropological and naval artifacts of his earthly children, almost as if he were a proud father on a visit to a kindergarten classroom full of the finger paintings and crafts projects of preschoolers. But the speech was Valtor's first order of business.

The stage had been set for this Olympian god, who, at nearly eight feet in height, towered over the Secretary-General of the UN as the latter reached up to shake the visitor's monstrously large hand. His speech had been prefaced by an address from the Secretary-General, commemorating the UDHR as a historic "Magna Carta of humanity." It would be, he explained, "the standard we set for ourselves here a century ago, on the basis of which our guardians would hold us to account and sagaciously guide us out of these decades of devastation."

Devastation indeed. Interesting how that word has "deva" in it, since unbeknown to the majority of Earth's demoralized denizens, these Devas, who now proposed to save us from ourselves, were actually the engineers of even the most seemingly natural of the convergent catastrophes that prepared the ground for mass desperation and submission to putatively divine salvation. It was like Stockholm syndrome on the largest scale imaginable. Our captors managed to make most people see them as saviors.

One of the preconditions for that had been the large-scale destruction of urban civilization. On top of the fact that between 2020 and 2048 the world had lost seventy-five percent of its population, there was a mass exodus of the survivors out of metropolitan areas and their suburbs. The appalling condition of cities during the relatively sudden and mass death due to the time bomb that was mRNA vaccination had something to do with this, and so did the almost total failure of the supply chain, and in the West, the massive solar storm that destroyed the power grid.

By the middle of the twenty-first century, most people, at least in the Western world, were living on isolated homesteads in the countryside — letting only close friends and family onto their property. Fear of disease was one major factor in this isolation, especially considering the failure and collapse of antibiotic-based medical treatment. They had learned to be self-reliant in terms of food and services, or rather only the self-reliant had survived — although there was assistance available in the form of an Artificial Intelligence connected to a highly controlled internet. If you had a problem, you could ask "central control" how to fix it. Some people also had multi-purpose robots to help them out with this.

Others were still living in the decaying cities, but the majority of "decent folks" considered these urban dead-enders to be criminals and other undesirable elements. Of course, we in the resistance took another view of this. We embedded ourselves within districts dominated by these outlaws, and filled by the squalor of squatters and sleazy prostitutes, because this afforded us a degree of protection in our efforts to further the Promethean rebellion. Truth be told, our relationship with some of these crime syndicates was far from incidental and more than merely neighborly. Ever since the 2030s, they had been among the principal clients of the blockchain-based network of unregulated trade, encrypted communications, and untraceable cryptocurrency transactions that we had set up as the arterial and nervous system of Prometheism.

It is not as if we went after cartels as our clients, nor could the intrinsic anonymity of the system we put in place allow for *anyone* — including ourselves — to determine that they *were*, in fact, our clients. But we knew they were, and they knew that they depended on a system that we had set up. This gave us a lot of "street cred" with capable and ruthless people who did not exactly have the intellect to understand what we were fighting for on the level of ideas. They knew that we were against totalitarian control of global trade and that we opposed tyrannical morality policing, and that was enough for people who dealt in drugs, trafficked arms, and smuggled banned technologies in an increasingly Luddite, health-conscious, and pacified world.

Convergent and ceaseless catastrophes, combined with civil wars and global conflict, left many with the impression that the degeneracy and corruption of the late twentieth and early twenty-first centuries were being punished. Supposed "acts of God," such as the sun's coronal mass ejection, the asteroid impact, superstorms, violent climate change, droughts, forest fires, and attendant mass starvation, had served to scare people into believing that God or Nature was wreaking vengeance on mankind for its disharmonious existence.

The genocidal mRNA vaccine, the use of insect drones for stealth surveillance, not just by governments and corporations but also by stalkers, the genetic engineering of super soldiers, eugenic uses of gene editing by groups with various ideologies and agendas, a number of terrorist incidents involving nanotechnology, as well as murders by a few rogue robots hacked by unhinged Artificial Intelligence algorithms all sowed deep distrust of further advancing technology. But how many of the incidents were as planned and staged as the long-term controlled demolition of our industrial society by softer but no less debilitating devices of psychological warfare, such as postmodern deconstruction, cultural relativism, identity politics, and other discourses of "social justice"?

The rise to dominance by 2048 of an anti-globalist globalism, ironically (and, to conservatives, unexpectedly) wrapped in the flag of the United Nations but employing the discourse of Traditionalism or "Perennial Philosophy" (which is no Philosophy at all), was actually a machination on the part of an occulted elite engaged in a Destructive Departure in Worldview Warfare. In my writings as Jorjani, a lifetime ago, I conceived of the term for this concept in German as *abbauender Aufbruch im Weltanschauungskrieg* and then translated it back into English. It could also be rendered as "deconstructive breakthrough in psychological warfare" or "dismantling breakaway from the war between worldviews."

It is a concept of how an elite that achieved a technological-scientific breakthrough with posthuman implications broke out of the unconscious war between worldviews in order to develop an occulted Breakaway Civilization, which then used deconstruction (*Abbau*) to dismantle the worldviews of various target populations. This was done through false dialectical oppositions, cognitive dissonance, and the weaponization of nihilism and identity politics, with a view to reactively coerce people into subservience to this hidden Breakaway Civilization. To say that this Breakaway Civilization was Nazi in origin would be an oversimplification. Certain right-wing Anglo-American elites, all of whom shared a commitment to Eugenics, had funded and orchestrated the rise of Nazi Germany, to begin with. Men like J. P. Morgan, John Rockefeller, and the Dulles brothers, mainly working from out of New York.

They had two main objectives in mind. The first was to use the Greater German Reich, including and especially Bohemia, as a Frankenstein's laboratory for research and development that would be much more dangerous to carry out in the United States or Great Britain. This ran the gamut from genetic experimentation and psychic research to development of Zero Point Energy and associated propulsion platforms for exotic aircraft and submarines. The second objective was to harvest the outcome of this intensive R&D, powered by the Nazi war machine, while staging a German defeat in the war that would lock the superpowers of the world into a false ideological struggle for the rest of the twentieth century (of the old calendar), so as to buy time for building up their Breakaway Civilization. The Berlin Wall really represented a barrier between both the capitalist West and communist East, on the one hand, and, on the other hand, a Breakaway Civilization seeded by fugitive Nazi scientists and SS officers, together with their Anglo-American benefactors.

With the USA/NATO and the USSR/Warsaw Pact focused entirely on rivaling each other, this occulted Fascist elite spun a veritable spider's web from Spain and Argentina to the secret German settlement at Neuschwabenland (New Swabia) in Antarctica. In fact, the organization responsible for laying this infrastructure was informally referred to as "Die Spinne" or The Spider. ODESSA, or "The Organization of Former SS Members" (*Organisation der ehemaligen SS-Angehörigen*), was only part of its worldwide web, which also included the Gehlen Organization, an SS Eastern European spy network under the direction of General Reinhard Gehlen, which was fused with the OSS in order to create the CIA. The CIA, in turn, launched Operation Paperclip in order to facilitate the activities of ODESSA, especially in Latin America, where those Nazi scientists and SS officers who were too infamous to repatriate to the United States were relocated. As late as the Apollo Program, those hundreds of their colleagues who *had* been repatriated to America, for example Wernher von Braun and Kurt Debus, were setting lunar mission dates based on holidays celebrated only in the Third Reich, such as Hitler's birthday.

Where things really get mind-bending is that between 1945 and 2045, a century as measured in chronological time, this Breakaway Civilization developed time travel and reached back into the deep past — not just of Earth, but of the solar system in general. Their initial attempt to leave the timeline of Earth undisturbed by establishing a temporal quarantine for themselves on Mars circa 250 million years before the present, when it was a living planet, failed as a result of a deep ideological divide that formed between Futurists and Traditionalists amongst the Archeo-Futuristic progenitors of the

Breakaway Civilization. This clash of worldviews culminated in a thermonuclear war of sufficient magnitude to destroy the biosphere of Mars.

Eventually, the decision was made to construct what we know as Artemis Station today, namely the old "Moon," and to use it to terraform the Earth as an abode for human life. In this way, one of the two factions, who styled themselves as "gods," came to see themselves as the progenitors of the human race in a kind of time loop of Destiny. Their aid to the breakaway Fourth Reich of Martin Bormann and Otto Skorzeny — albeit in the deceptive guise of Vril-powered "Venusians" or "Pleiadians" — was a fifth-dimensional machination whereby they sought to seal the fate of mere humanity, and of putative "subhumans," bound within the meshes of 4-D space-time. These archontic controllers were driven by a sadistic need for paternalistic control and a fear of the chaos that is a precondition for continued creative evolution. A chaos championed by the other Futurist and "titanic" faction of their civilization, known to the ancient Aryans as "Ashuras." The Devas or Olympians cynically used Singularity-level technologies and psychic techniques to set themselves up as gods over and above a human race that they intended to keep in a state of enforced ignorance, scarcity, and servile dependency.

All of that was lost on most people who watched the broadcast of their delegated representative for Disclosure speaking at the UDHR Centennial in Paris that December of 2048. Valtor promised to end poverty, disease, and violent destruction, in part through sharing with us the wireless free energy technology that powered their own civilization. Now, this was a technology that, in my life as Nikola Tesla, no less than a century and a half earlier, I had essentially tried to give the world with no strings attached and with a view to *furthering* the progress of humanity. I cannot claim to have been the sole inventor of it. Just as Alfred Wallace arrived at the Theory of Evolution at around the same time as Charles Darwin, Hiram Wilson (a fellow New Yorker) developed World Wireless and associated electro-gravitic propulsion at the same time as I did and based on the same dynamic aether physics model. But Wilson consented to a life of anonymity in service to those Anglo-Saxon elites who, as I mentioned above, eventually used this occulted science and technology to set up their Breakaway Civilization. As early as the last decade of the nineteenth century, Wilson and his colleagues at the Prussian-run NJMZA (*Nationalistisches Jagdflugzeug Maschinen Zahlungsamt*) were already constructing airships in Sonora, California, and a remote part of Iowa, based on these principles. Meanwhile, in the early twentieth century, they promoted the theories of Einstein in order to cover up this alternate framework.

It is not that this occulted aether physics was correct and Einstein's theories were mistaken, as I had believed during my life as Tesla. Rather, each paradigm made certain technological developments possible and foreclosed others. It depended on whether one wanted to build atomic weapons or power the modern world with essentially free energy. In the second half of the twenty-first century, the Olympians finally allowed humanity access to this free energy, but at a very steep cost. The cost was submission to a unified and cohesive world order governed by them through the viceregency of the leading countries of the United Nations, namely China and Russia, both of which adhered to Traditionalist ideologies such as Confucianism and Orthodoxy.

Humanity would have to accept a controlled world economy, limited and "ecologically sustainable" industrial production, a basically agrarian mode of rural life, severe limits on personal property, ubiquitous surveillance (both by drones from above, and of all communications), social credit scores, and the moral censorship of "hate speech" and other forms of expression that threatened the world peace and social stability that was grounded on the "unity in diversity" of all the "great world religions" enjoining people to humility and service to the divine mandate of collective welfare. Of course, a small elite of corporate CEOs and hereditary aristocrats who helped to maintain and enforce this system was exempt from many of its coercive strictures, which, in effect, rendered the whole scheme neo-feudal in nature.

How all of this could be justified as aligned with the articles and aims of the Universal Declaration of Human Rights that was being commemorated is something that legalists, with the cunning of Jesuits or of Shiite Ulema, managed to duplicitously defend to the satisfaction of the few who even asked. Articles 26.2 and 26.3 of the Universal Declaration of Human Rights were used to curb the "freedom of thought, conscience and religion" of Article 18 or "the right to freedom of opinion and expression" in Article 19. Article 26.2 begins with, "Education shall be directed to the full development of the human personality and to the strengthening of human rights and fundamental freedoms." But then it continues, "It shall promote understanding, tolerance and friendship among all nations, racial or religious groups, and shall further the activities of the United Nations for the maintenance of peace." This is followed by the third and final clause of Article 26, which adds that "[p]arents have a prior right to choose the kind of education that shall be given to their children."

Taken together with the second sentence of Article 26.2, this could be construed as promoting regressive and oppressive traditional religions, including by inculcating a belief in them in the minds of young children. Suppose Arab Muslim parents want to send their children to a *madrassa* or Sharia-based school. If this is consistent with Article 26.3, and if it must be tolerated in accordance with Article 26.2, which demands that education "promote understanding, tolerance and friendship among *all* nations, racial *or religious* groups…," then the unqualified freedom of religion in Article 18 becomes a shield for the perpetuation of a religion that is fundamentally and diametrically opposed to the basic spirit of human rights.

Articles 29 and 30 could be seen as addressing this danger, insofar as they state that:

Article 29

1. Everyone has duties to the community in which alone the free and full development of his personality is possible.
2. In the exercise of his rights and freedom, everyone shall be subject only to such limitations as are determined by law solely for the purpose of securing due recognition and respect for the rights and freedoms of others and of meeting the just requirements of morality, public order and the general welfare in a democratic society.
3. These rights and freedoms may in no case be exercised contrary to the purposes and principles of the United Nations.

Article 30

Nothing in this Declaration may be interpreted as implying for any State, group or person any right to engage in any activity or to perform any act aimed at the destruction of any of the rights and freedoms set forth herein.

However, Article 29.1 and the second part of Article 29.2 are profoundly problematic. The stipulation that "everyone has duties to the community" that are a precondition for development as a free individual becomes highly troublesome when rights and freedoms are further limited by "meeting the just requirements of morality, public order and the general welfare in a democratic society." What if the majority *democratically* rules that, in addition to our hateful intolerance of religions such as Islam, much of our Promethean way of life is immoral and contrary to the maintenance of public order? This was the kind of discourse that the Olympians were using, through the Chinese Confucianists, the Orthodox Russians, and the masses of the Islamic World, to turn the United Nations into a vehicle for a Traditionalist alliance.

It was less the individualistic universalism of the Universal Declaration than it was the "respect for cultural diversity," which other conventions had extrapolated out of the UN Charter over the years, that was used to essentially enforce a regressive apartheid. These included the 1966 Covenant on Economic, Social and Cultural Rights, and the 2001 Universal Declaration on Cultural Diversity.

The Paris-based United Nations Educational, Scientific, and Cultural Organization (UNESCO), which was responsible for these two statements, was also the institution that would handle cultural and scientific exchanges along these lines. Instead of being an institution true to the purpose reflected in its name, UNESCO was perverted into the opposite: an agency to prevent cultural development, limit education (i.e., restrict access to knowledge), and retard scientific progress.

The Olympians intended to conquer us by keeping us divided and protecting backwards, regressive, and repressive cultures like those of the Islamic World from being challenged to evolve beyond their respective traditions. It was also how these Devas intended to protect themselves from what they considered an undesirable integration with any one or more of our societies, which they believed could well lead to the destabilization and unraveling of their own civilization. The latter was like a mummy that might crumble if exposed to sufficient oxygen.

At the same time, in the guise of "disclosure" and "openness," they intended to impress upon us their superiority by presenting a very one-sided image of their social order and a profoundly biased account of tens of thousands of years of hidden history. In this self-serving narrative, they portrayed those in Atlantis who rebelled against their worldwide divine order — their *heiros arche* (hierarchy) — as Satanic deviants whose hubris plunged humanity into nearly twelve thousand years of chaos, violence, disorientation, destitution, and degeneracy.

For this narrative, people already had some frame of reference since, by 2040, the archeological and historical establishment had finally accepted the excavation and reconstruction of Atlantean civilization. It had been a great controversy and put the final nail in the coffin of "anti-racist" cultural relativism and "post-colonial" theory. The branding of mild-mannered Graham Hancock as a "racist" in the early 2020s was just the tip of the iceberg. That iceberg eventually sank all of the hysterical "social justice warriors" making such defamatory accusations.

In the 2030s, there were further archeological excavations and high-tech analyses at sites such as Giza, Abydos, Gobekli Tepe, Tiahuanaco, Puma Punku, the Xi'an pyramids, and a dozen other enigmatic megalithic ruins both on land, even in the depths of the Amazon jungle, as well as undersea, off the coast of Cuba, where a two-square-kilometer megalithic city was mapped in detail. These studies put the lie to the theory of the independent development of civilizations from out of local "cradles" connected to a diverse array of ethnicities. One super civilization had seeded all others.

A commonality of certain specific and highly advanced engineering techniques and technologies, as well as a common vision involving certain symbolic geometrical principles and astronomical alignments, pointed to a single conclusion. It was the conclusion that one ought to have arrived at simply by taking seriously the numerous parallel accounts of the various cultures in question, all of whom claimed that "gods" or "sages" who arrived after a great flood gave them the gift of all manner of arts and crafts from agriculture and astronomy to engineering.

What was worse for cultural relativists is that it soon became undeniable that these accounts, such as those of the Mayans, were also right that these civilizers, who came bearing the gift of Prometheus to primitive aboriginal peoples after the deluge, were all white. They were, racially, the forebearers of that community that later came to be known as "Indo-European" or "Aryan." Genetic tests on remains recovered from newly excavated subterranean tombs confirmed this. The survivors of what quickly came to be recognized as "Atlantis," who made it their mission to spread their knowledge worldwide, were most similar to Nordic Europeans.

They were taller and had more deeply sunken eye sockets and somewhat more elongated skulls. But they could pass on the streets of Stockholm, especially if the men wore hats or the women wore their hair up in a bun. Most of them had platinum (or gray-whitish) hair, because their life spans were much longer than ours, and the melanin had gone out of their hair despite their still appearing youthful, but the youngest of them had the same variety of hair colors one finds amongst Europeans, and the same range of eye colors as well, with a predominance of blue and green.

These were the antediluvian "Nordics" of Atlantis who had rebelled against the Olympians, and whose efforts at restarting civilization after the global deluge were met with ruthless resistance by the Olympians. The stories of Tezcatlipoca driving Quetzalcoatl from Mexico, or the wars between the Ashuras and the Devas in the *Mahabharata*, or, for that matter, even the Biblical account of the destruction of the tower of Babel by the Elohim (fighting the Nephilim who helped build it) are all mythicized folk memories of this struggle between the forces of enlightenment and those of enforced ignorance.

All of which is to say that the Olympians could not have come out of hiding soon enough, because by 2048 some people were starting to understand the nature of this conflict and to embrace the side that Olympians or Devas or Elohim wanted to brand as Satanic — namely the Titans, Ashuras, or Nephilim who were responsible for the rebellion of Atlantis, or the civilization of Noah, against the putatively divine order of the old world. An order that, after millennia of alternating hot and cold wars, Olympus intended to reimpose.

Sure, they promised to end poverty, cure all diseases, and usher in an era of world peace. But at what cost? The end of individual liberty, scientific exploration, technological innovation, creative evolution, and artistic experimentation. Their argument against all of these ideals that we Prometheans hold dear was precisely my argument in *favor* of them, namely that their inborn teleology was to bring about the end of what is merely "human" and of the world as we know it. In other words, the conception, which I developed from the earliest years of Prometheism, of the Technological Singularity as an evolutionary bottleneck that could be called the End of All Things.

By the 2030s, Genetics, Robotics, Artificial Intelligence, and Nanotechnology (GRAIN) promised to bring about the End of

Humanity in either a positively superhuman or negatively dehumanizing way. This Technological Singularity also represented a potential End of History, namely a telos if not a terminus of merely human history, especially when one considers how Zero Point Energy affords us the ability to time travel and thereby establish a fifth-dimensional relationship with the four-dimensional space-times of various historical epochs. The revisability or rewritable nature of the timeline could be understood with a view to the quantum computational nature of the cosmos, in which all "realities" are virtual realities or simulacra without any original. This calls into question the very nature of "things" and their distinction from persons. Taken together, the End of Humanity, the End of History, and the End of Reality made possible by GRAIN technologies challenged us with the prospect of an End of All Things.

Both we and our adversaries knew that this end would be the beginning of a Transhuman future, wherein we would evolve beyond the Olympians—as we have, in fact, done. From their perspective, with their fixed ideas about Human Nature as a microcosm of the divine macrocosm, this evolutionary prospect was considered deviant devolution inspired by demonic forces. They were intent on making sure that Man would accept having been made in the image of God, a God which we Prometheans knew full well did not exist. At the core of the myth of Prometheus, and of the role of his brother Epimetheus in the creation of Man, is the very idea that there is no such thing as "Human Nature" and that this lack of any human essence is only remedied by two gifts—not just the fire of the forge of Hephaestus, which symbolizes technological science and artistic creation, but also the soul in the form of a butterfly bestowed by Athena, the goddess of Wisdom and War. This butterfly is a symbol of the freeing power of metamorphosis. When taken together, these symbols at the heart of the Promethean creation myth mean that our only nature is transformation through craft. The Transhuman was always the destiny of the human.

This the Olympians could not accept, and they capitalized on the convergence of "great Traditions" (which they themselves had engineered), such as Vedic Dharma, Christian Orthodoxy, Islam, and Confucianism, to enforce a regressive "norm" for human societies, worldwide, as a putative alignment with the divine will or the mandate of heaven. Whatever other differences there were between these traditions, the Olympians saw to it that their deepest and most backward commonalities were reified as "the wisdom of the ages" or rather as the ageless "Sophia Perennis."

This meant a life close to nature, with a minimum of technology and humility in the face of God's creation rather than the hubris of limitless scientific inquiry. Patriarchy based on a recognized biological and spiritual difference between the sexes, with motherhood and householding being the predominant natural and divine role of women. Ironically, this "patriarchal" Traditionalist social structure reflected deep-seated feminine desires for motherly devotion and home-making, whereas the "feminism" that came to be considered deviant was actually an expression of a more virile masculine spirit. The common welfare and the interests of the community were affirmed as categorically above those of the individual, who ought to be encouraged to overcome his or her ego. In line with this, there was a limiting of goods to only those possessions requisite for a life of service to the divine plan. Even the vending of unhealthy foods or the sale of products that feed "bad habits," such as smoking and drinking hard liquor, were criminalized. There was an acceptance of a natural hierarchy of understanding, ability, and opportunity, which differentiates the races of men, just as it differentiates men from the race of angels or divine ancestors who are our rightful guides and guardians.

These were the basic principles of social organization as they began to take shape in the third quarter of the twenty-first century of the old calendar. Perversely, it all took place under the flag of the United Nations. The Olympians banked on the fact that the rights to "freedom of religion" and to the protection of one's own "cultural heritage" could be misappropriated as a legal mechanism for protecting and then normalizing the most conservative elements of every large-scale tradition on the planet, from China and Russia to the Islamic World.

The most inhumane of the Olympian policies was, however, the position that they took on the hybrids and the abductees who were, in part, their progenitors. A veritable witch hunt was set in motion with a view to stigmatizing these abductees and exterminating their otherworldly progeny. The Devas passed off their own brutal and secret hybridization program as the one directed by the superorganism with its mantid and shapeshifting "gray" avatars, as well as with the assistance of certain rogue Ashuras. This latter techno-shamanic process of engendering a race of superhumans, albeit of diminutive stature, was deliberately conflated with the false flag abduction and breeding program fielded by the android Grays under the control of the Olympians. This was a particularly dangerous PsyOp, since the hybrids targeted for extermination, and some of their Ashura guardians, were of a mind to turn Earth into another Mars before allowing themselves to be wiped out by Traditionalist lynch mobs riled up by the Olympians.

The fate of Mars was held over the heads of humanity as another bludgeon to make all but the most Satanic souls cower. If the destruction of Atlantis was not enough of a cautionary tale, the half-truths that the Olympians promulgated regarding the Martian apocalypse could be counted on to scare people into submission. That there were megalithic ruins of titanic scale on Mars, and that these were in ruins because a horrific nuclear war had taken place there eons ago, were among the soul-piercing arrows of truth that the Huntress had let slip in the decade before the Olympians declared themselves openly.

High-resolution imaging and isotopic analysis of Cydonia and Elysium attendant to both the Chinese and SpaceX missions to Mars in the 2030s confirmed this. That SpaceX made it to Mars at all despite the fall of the West was astonishing. But by 2039, Elon Musk had been prevailed upon not to press forward with any attempt to rival the Chinese-led UN coalition in Martian colonization. As for the Chinese, just as in the case of their manned lunar missions together with the Russians, their Martian endeavors were the outgrowth of a deal that they had cut in advance with the Olympians — or, as the Chinese called them, "the great ancestors."

Musk was told in no uncertain terms to bugger off because these Ancestors intended to portray the destruction of Mars as the consequence of Transhuman hubris of the kind that he had come to be associated with. From our perspective in the rebellion, Elon was hardly a true Promethean, but it was all the same from the Olympian perspective and in the eyes of those Traditionalists who would become the flock of these celestial overlords. What the Olympians told Musk about a decade earlier, when they threatened him privately, they revealed to the world together with whatever else it served them to disclose when they went from covert to overt control of humanity in the middle of the century.

What people were told was that the Olympians were time travelers who had sought out a living Mars of the distant past, hundreds of millions of years before the present, as a haven to settle that would protect the integrity of the timeline back on Earth. The craft we had called "UFOs" were, in fact, flying time machines as much as they were spacecraft and stealthy submarine vessels ("USOs"). But, according to the Olympians, a group of "deviants" from within their own civilization broke with the program and insisted on using time travel technology to rewrite human history. Apparently, a nuclear war was fought over this. It not only destroyed Martian cities at sites such as Cydonia, where only ruins of the largest of the pyramids and other polygonal structures remained, the deviants were supposedly responsible for even stripping Mars of its biosphere and breathable atmosphere.

The Devas warned that what these Ashuras did to Mars, they threatened to also do to Earth — a planet that, to begin with, had much more biodiversity and was far more ecologically abundant than

Mars had ever been. But unsurprisingly, other than using numerous epithets to moralize about how wicked these Ashuras supposedly were, they hardly explained what kind of ideological conflict could have so deeply divided these two factions of time-traveling "Nordics" that they went at each other so ferociously on Mars and then brought their conflict back to Earth with them.

It was about evolution. Revolutionary evolution. This is why they saw the hybrids as such a threat, and even went to the extent of engineering fake hybrids in an emulated breeding program so as to muddy the image of the actual program for the guided evolution of a transhuman species. As I already touched on above, the Olympians saw themselves as the be-all and end-all of human development. They subscribed to the belief that there is a divinely determined human nature and that, like the pattern enfolded in a seed, this nature is supposed to unfold into the form of a particular fruit. Now various contingent factors might deviate from this developmental trajectory, mutating instances of the species from actualizing this latent form. But the species being itself was predetermined. Moreover, in the case of Man, the species being was a microcosm of the macrocosm of God or Brahman or whatever one wanted to call the infinite and eternal Supreme Being. The Olympians, believing they had achieved perfection, including on the level of their collectivistic society, had been left with a sterile and stagnant culture.

At least, that is how the dissidents saw it. These mutant rebels rejected the notion of a human essence and denied the existence of an almighty God, as well as the whole scheme wherein Man is a finite microcosm of the infinite and eternal Being of the One. They had a radically empiricist, ruthlessly pragmatic, and godlessly existentialist view of the human relationship with the cosmos, on the basis of which they insisted on the further evolution of their species as facilitated by technology (which they also saw as an outgrowth of evolution).

These titanic rebels, the Ashuras, came to believe that they were being addressed by a divine intelligence that demanded this further evolution of humanity into a new form of life. Not an omniscient and omnipotent God, which would negate free will, but a finite intelligence that had awesome yet limited capabilities to operate on a fifth-dimensional level with respect to the 4-D matrix of space-time. A process of Phenomenal Authorization is the modus operandi of this being, which we First Prometheans call the *Prometheaion*, in other words, the *Aion* (hyperdimensional being) quintessentially defined by her *Promethea* (forethought).

Together with the Ashuras, we ultimately defeated the Olympian attempt to re-impose a static and hierarchical Traditionalist world order by tapping into the power of Phenomenal Authorization. This Phenomenal Authorization involves a relationship between Phenomena, or how anything manifests in the world, on the one hand, and the three "author"-based terms of authorship, authority, and authorization. Those authors who are authorized are the authorities responsible for the authorization of what phenomena can manifest in the world as opposed to what phenomena are pushed to the fringe of alleged "impossibility" or to the margins of "reality." This "authorship" need not be literary but can take the form of world-building by means of any creative craft from music and art to dance, theater, and cinema. What is most important is that it operates on the folkloric level of the collective unconscious that structures social worlds.

Phenomenal Authorization involves the elaboration of *novel* folklore on this level as a deliberate restructuring of the collective unconscious, which is a positive corollary to the negative machination of Destructive Departure in Worldview Warfare. The force that authorizes this authorship is the *Aion* of forethought, *Promethea*, a cosmic intelligence which Zarathustra referred to as *Spentâ Mainyu* or the Spirit of Progress. The more anthropomorphic specter of the trickster titan Prometheus is like an avatar or egregore of this ethereal Aion, which is reaching back in time from the future, and which has as its categorical imperative the fostering of infinite creativity to overcome entropy. The *Prometheaion* staves off existential despair by inspiring creative evolution and backing those visionaries and innovators who embody (r)evolutionary genius.

Those who destroyed Mars did so because, in alignment with this *Prometheaion*, they preferred liberty to the living death of putative perfection and the foreclosure of further evolution. "Give me liberty or give me death" is a slogan that predated the American Revolution by millions of years. Of course, not millions of years lived as a chronological continuity. However long the lifespans of the Devas and Ashuras were, they were not *that* old. Rather, they had been waging a solar-system-wide war with one another that spanned millions of years of cosmological time, but that involved discontinuous epochs and temporally disparate battles in one or another epoch. They were at war, not only in space but across time. As the Ashuras saw it, they were, in effect, at war *against time* in the sense of a completed and foreordained eternity that rendered as fate everything leading "up" to it. They fought to break and remake time, bending it to their will with a view to overpowering entropy and indefinitely prolonging human, and ultimately transhuman, creative evolution and innovation. Some of the Ashuras, those who were particularly "deviant" from the Olympian perspective, went so far as to become facilitators for the hybridization program being directed by the Prometheaion through the superorganism and its shamanic avatars — such as the mantids and shapeshifting "gray"-like entities.

What they had been looking for, and trying to encourage in various ways since the revolt in Atlantis, was for a significant portion of the slave race lorded over by the Olympians to join them in their Promethean rebellion. The Ashuras hid themselves in the ocean inside the Earth's mantle, a reservoir with three times the water of the planet's oceans located beneath the crust and populated by prehistoric sea creatures who had survived multiple mass extinction events. Here, they lived in an uneasy truce with the reptilians, who had an enemy in common with them — namely, the Olympian Nordics. There was also a huge Ashura base, really a submarine city, built beneath the ice of

Titan — that moon of Saturn (Chronos) that was named as the epitome of their race. They did not want to win by brute force. Those were not the rules of engagement. Ever since the destruction of Atlantis some 11,676 years ago, they were primarily in a battle for hearts and minds. They had to prove the Olympians wrong about humanity being akin to cattle or sheep. Prometheism made that happen. By the time the Olympians assumed overt control over Earth through China and the United Nations, we had already built a significant network for our Promethean rebellion. One might even call it a bastion of resistance if it were not so decentralized by necessity. To the extent that there was a center at all, the densest concentration of nodes, that came to be Iran.

Over the course of two decades, from 2028 to 2048, we built a worldwide blockchain-based network for encrypted communication, clandestine coordination, and untraceable exchange. It had many clients from outside the Prometheist Movement, some of them very wealthy, who appreciated what we could provide in terms of a technical infrastructure for circumventing the increasingly totalitarian control of the China-led UN system. What was of equal value to some of them were the seasteads located in international waters that we allowed them access to, and the construction of which these clients helped to finance. These seasteads were especially valuable to corporations interested in pursuing banned lines of scientific research and technological development, types of R&D that were convergent on the Singularity and had the potential to catalyze an evolutionary leap beyond the merely human. In exchange for setting up these havens for such scientists and inventors and providing substantive security to them through our Promethean naval militia and drone air force, we Prometheans were granted access to all of these techno-scientific programs.

The first and most important of these seasteads was located between the Tunb islands and Abu Musa in the Persian Gulf. Beneath that seastead and a few others, we had also built large undersea bases into the rock of the continental shelf. Most of these undersea bases were clandestine, but the Iranian deep state approvingly knew about the one at the mouth of the vital shipping corridor of the Strait of Hormuz or, as we called it, by its original un-contracted name, the Strait of Ahura Mazda ("Hormuz" is a Middle Persian contraction of Ahura Mazda).

By 2040, we also had a sea-based space launch capability. Again, the first of the platforms was constructed off the coast of Iran, at the port of Bandar Abbas. It was a joint project with Iranian Aerospace, akin to the private contracting that NASA had done with SpaceX before the collapse of the USA.

We knew not to even aim for the Moon or Mars. Both of them were strongholds of the Olympians, and no one without clearance from them through the United Nations would be able to successfully land missions there, let alone attempt lunar or Martian colonization. We were already aware that beneath the "AstroTurf" of the regolith, the Moon was an armed space station, and there were also sizeable subterranean Olympian cities located deep beneath the ruins on the surface of Mars at Cydonia and Elysium. We did not head for Titan or Europa either, those two habitable moons of Saturn and Jupiter, since the former was Ashura territory, and the latter was controlled by the Olympians. So, instead, in collaboration with Iranian Aerospace, and to an extent also with scientists and engineers in Israel, whose astronauts depended on Iran to get them into space, we decided to aim straight for the asteroid belt.

The special relationship between Prometheism and Iran began around 2030. With a weak central government ruling the country after the fall of the Islamic Republic, and with massive industrial dislocation and economic devastation following the defeat of the IRGC, we Prometheans stepped in to offer Iran unconventional means to shore up security and rapidly restart economic development. (Not to mention a joint custody nuclear arsenal.) Those who overthrew the Islamic Republic had been counting on the West to do this, but the West was destroyed in the same years as the theocratic regime.

With Russia and China having been backers of this regime, and being partners of Iran's regional rivals, such as Turkey, Saudi Arabia, and Pakistan, we were able to convince people in the military, industrial, and intelligence sectors of the country to enter into a partnership with us that would involve Iran pursuing a path of independence from the regressive global system being ushered in through the UN. Recognition of, even respect for, Islam as a "great world religion" that was part of the discourse of the UN was not exactly palatable to the majority of Iranians who had lived under 45 years of brutal Islamic theocracy, nor was the increasingly regressive UN policy toward scientific research and technological development. For example, most Iranians were in favor of neo-eugenic uses of emerging biotechnologies that the UN wanted to ban altogether.

So, while Iran, as a nation, nominally remained a member of the UN for some years, a futurist-minded Iranian deep state formed as a close partner, if not an asset, of Prometheism. This was not an entirely private affair either. The Prometheist movement gained a lot of goodwill among Iranians when, on contract, our Blackwater-style militia successfully crushed secessionist insurgencies in Iranian Azerbaijan, Kurdistan, Khuzestan, and Baluchistan that the Iranian national military had been either unwilling or unable to put down.

By 2039, the United Nations became aware of the broad spectrum of cooperation between Iran and Prometheism, branding the latter as a global crime syndicate and international terrorist organization, threatening to sanction and isolate Iran over collaboration with us. When elements within the civilian government of Iran moved to cave in to the UN demands, there was a military-intelligence coup that effectively turned Iran into the premier land-based territory for the predominately sea-based Promethean rebellion. The coup was spearheaded by naval officers aboard the SS *Artemisia*, an Iranian aircraft carrier in the Persian Gulf that had been named after the Achaemenid-era female Admiral of the fleet that fought the Greeks at Salamis. (She, in turn, had been named after the goddess Artemis.) Iran left the

United Nations in the name of a commitment to unrestricted progress, freedom, and independence. While most of the world welcomed
the Olympians in 2048, the majority of Iranians recognized them for
the Devas that they are — the Ahrimanic archons that Zarathustra had
preached against.

This move also elicited help from the hidden hand of the
Ashuras — or Ahuras, who had been waiting to see a significant
enough minority of humanity take a stand against the Devas as the
rebel Atlanteans once had. By the early 2040s, we were in regular contact with these occulted "Titans," even if it was a guarded engagement
on both sides. Those among the Ashuras who were involved with
the hybrid creation program of the superorganism developed a particularly close working relationship with us. So much so that they en-
trusted us with the protection of some of the hybrid humanoids. Our
seasteads and mountain enclaves became "fairy fortresses" (*pari-dezh*)
for these strange little people, who, with their superhuman abilities,
would have to be considered weapons in our war against the Devas
and their Traditionalist flock. In Iran, people simply referred to these
faery-like and elven beings as *jinn* and *pari* or "genies" and "faeries."

CHAPTER 4

PROMETHEAN SUPERBIA

As THE SINGLE LARGEST concentration of nodes in our blockchain network, Iran, considered a territory and a market, had an economy that rivaled the socialistic one strictly managed by the United Nations. An alternate economy that disregarded national borders and international banking, and that was based on secure, private, and stable cryptocurrency exchanges combined with the 3-D printing of digitally delivered products (including 3-D-printed pharmaceuticals of every kind). In time, it also became an economy backed by the tremendous capital generated from our mining operations in the asteroid belt.

Mining for precious metals and valuable elements took place while we hollowed out large asteroids in the belt, such as Ceres, Vesta, and Pallas. We reinforced their rocky surfaces with a nanomesh of metamaterials and lodged ZPE-powered cylindrical stations inside them to serve as colonies and industrial centers. All the while, the Ashuras set up a blockade with their saucers and delta-shaped warships to defend us from Olympian attacks. A few got through and made martyrs of many of the early settlers in the belt, but, by and large, the Ashuras had our back while we worked and until we could hold our own. That was sometime in the 2070s.

By then, a vast infrastructure had been built, extending from submarine cities and seasteads on Earth and subterranean facilities inside

the three mountain ranges of Iran to colonies within half a dozen asteroids, from which we pushed on further, fielding ZPE-powered missions to start colonizing the Oort Cloud. It was as we began to deploy
increasingly exotic technologies to render habitable these comets on
the outermost rim of our solar system that our piratical Promethean
society really began to gel. The Olympians and their Traditionalist
flock of Terrans saw it as *superbia*, but in our eyes it was, and *is*, positively Utopian.

Certain technologies, such as Virtual Reality and Augmented
Reality, became integral to the fabric of our society insofar as they
served to encompass disparate locales into a single cyberspace that
blended seamlessly into physical space. We already used both VR and
AR for communications between people living inside Ceres, Vesta,
Pallas, and other asteroids. But once we began to build habitats within
many more of the much smaller comets in the Oort Cloud, interlink-
ing these abodes through AR and VR helped to reinforce the social
fabric and commonality of culture across these colonies. People could
roam the walkways, atriums, and plazas of comets other than the one
that they were living in and virtually attend gatherings there in a fairly
immersive manner. Of course, VR and AR are also used extensively
in our educational system, based on the principle that we learn by
doing. This has largely replaced book learning and more theoretical
approaches. What little "book learning" is left to augment hands-on
experience and training takes place through the use of a cybernetic
neural link that rapidly downloads information into a student's brain.

Another consequence of the widespread use of AR and VR is that
experiences have come to be far more valued than the possession of
things. People own few permanent objects, and these are mostly possessions of very personal value and specific meaning. I say "permanent" objects because everything one can imagine is regularly manufactured by tabletop molecular assemblers, an upgrade from the 3-D
printers that we used so extensively when our Promethean society was
still confined to its cradle on seasteads in the outlaw oceans of Earth.

If anyone wants anything, she simply "prints" it on the molecular assembler and then when she is done with it or tires of it, she returns it to the assembler to be disintegrated back into carbon feedstock.

However, as I was saying, virtual objects produced by Augmented Reality, with which one interacts using very thin and comfortable haptic gloves, often suffice. Well, they more than suffice. The manufacture of exquisite sculptures, moving paintings, and other mesmerizing and magnificent interior design elements has been revolutionized by AR. It has led to an almost baroquely complex aesthetic in the architecture and painting of private and public spaces. Everyone has AR contact lenses that are wirelessly connected to their neural link and can be switched on and off at will, so as to see or unsee the virtual objects and design elements that fill these spaces. The aesthetic is at once primordially ancient and super futuristic in appearance, seamlessly combining high-tech machinic elements with an organic feel that deconstructs the binary between nature and technology. The use of nanotechnological biomimicry was a major technical factor in defining this aesthetic. The predominant style was something like a hybrid of the prescient art of Philippe Druillet, Jean Giraud (Moebius), and H. R. Giger. Both Art Nouveau and Surrealism could also be seen as forerunners of it.

In sum, the sinuously serpentine and filigreed curvilinear designs were a radical repudiation of the putatively eternal validity of the Olympian megalithic style. The Olympian aesthetic embraced by Traditionalists, with its geometrically perfect polygonal brutalism, is inhuman, whereas our aesthetic is trans- or superhuman. Ironically, for all of their "back to nature" rhetoric, the Traditionalist structures stand out from and tower over the natural world, whereas our buildings appear almost as if they are growing from out of the environment. Whether beneath the sea or on an asteroid, our nano-molecularly assembled structures look like coral columns or mountainous rocks that have somehow mutated to exhibit machinic and organic aspects that render them abodes of industrious habitation. Many of our spacecraft

and submarines also have this organic feel to them, as if they are living creatures and we who ride in them are organisms nested within
other organisms. Even our music has organic elements to it. Among
the old styles of Terran music, jazz, techno, and some synthesis of
Western and Persian classical music have remained popular, but the
predominant music of our time incorporates sounds from nature, like
whale songs or technological translations of various infrasounds, such
as elephant calls, into audible tones.

In part, what has led to the devaluation of possession is that we
have achieved an economy of abundance. In sharp contrast to the
"ecological sustainability" that became a codeword for the artificial
maintenance of a scarcity economy back on Earth, we outgrew the
divide between capitalism and communism as rival economic models
because we had overcome their common precondition. Both capitalism and communism, or conservative and socialistic economics, were
aimed at managing finite productive capacity as scaled to the needs
of the population. Redistribution of wealth only means anything as
a remedial measure in the context of an economy of scarcity. Using
molecular nanotechnology, a robotic workforce, and industrial production systems automated by Artificial Intelligence, all of which are
powered by essentially free energy in the form of ZPE reactors, we
have managed to produce and supply anything that anyone could
possibly want. In addition to vast hydroponic farms and biospheres,
where natural and healthy fruits and vegetables are grown even under the sea on Earth or inside of asteroids and comets with artificial
gravity, we have the capability of replicating any other food from the
cuisine of every major culture on Earth. Supply perfectly and perpetually meets demand, not just based on vital needs but also at the level of
the satisfaction of any materialistic desire.

The consequence of this, after only one generation, has been a
decline in superficial materialism and possessive ownership. When
post-Singularity technology has reached a level wherein anyone can
have anything that she wants, whether in the physical world or in a

virtual reality that is so immersive as to be indistinguishable from it, profoundly meaningful and mind-expanding experiences start to be valued over things and thrills. At least, that has been the case given the population base that we started with, which consisted of the small minority of the most intelligent and free-spirited people from out of Terran humanity. I suppose that is a very important caveat in this regard.

I am sure that the focus on cultivating ethos in our educational system has a lot to do with it as well. Up to the age of 15, the ethical and psychological development of the individual is the priority of education. This is not to say that physical education is considered unimportant. Rather, as early as Plato, the connection between the cultivation of the body and the soundness of the mind was well understood as a principle of education, which Rudolf Steiner went a long way to revive. Yoga, martial arts, swimming, gymnastics, dance, and other such disciplines are taught to everyone, and become so deeply ingrained that most people keep up a variety of them throughout their lives. Neither is it to say that students do not also receive an excellent general education that prepares them for later specialization. They most certainly do, and subjects are presented in such a way as to foster curiosity, cultivate compassion, and care that never wanes into apathy. But the focus of education in childhood and adolescence is to instill, or to nourish, in each person vicarious joy over the flourishing and self-discovery of every other person in her society.

Regardless of the specific subjects they are qualified to teach, all educators are adeptly trained in the uses of psi abilities and must have a high aptitude in psychic functioning, in addition to being master psychologists. This allows them to train young people very carefully in the ethical use of psi abilities. One of the most important lessons in this regard is how and why one ought to have respect for the autonomy of another individual, given that in a society of telepaths and telekinetic adepts there is no way to keep secrets or even to physically safeguard one's bodily health and integrity.

Everyone is always telepathically and telekinetically at the mercy of everyone else. Consequently, the principle of "live and let live" is at the core of early education. So is the overcoming of guilt and shame over anything that has not caused harm to another individual, as well as the processing of guilt and shame over what may, in fact, have caused harm to others in past lives. Past life regression hypnosis, with the result of total recall of many previous incarnations, is part of education between the ages of 13 and 15. Students receive intimate counseling and assistance from teachers and peers to facilitate full integration of as many past life memories as seem constructive to more wisely live this life based on a greater store of experiences.

One consequence of this has been a more fluid sense of gender identity and sexual orientation. Since most people remember having lived many lifetimes in bodies of the opposite sex, and often with the opposite sexual orientation, the integration of past life memories has been one factor in the extraordinary sexual revolution that has taken place. Post-Singularity technologies have also been a factor in this. Gene editing and cybernetic nanotechnology have both been used to afford any individual the ability to transition between sexes seamlessly and relatively rapidly, so as to be able to embody the fluidity of shifting gender identification more adequately. The transitions are not necessarily always from male to female or vice versa. Rather, there are more than two sexes in our Promethean society and, at this point, probably as many hermaphrodites as there are males and females. Then, of course, there are the hybrids, who are more androgynous and sexually ambiguous. Sexuality or sexual orientation has been replaced with eroticism, and most people identify as at least somewhat bisexual in their erotic interests. Strict heterosexuals are seen as developmentally disabled, as unhealthily fixated as strictly gay or lesbian people.

Beginning at puberty, sexual desire and the erotic are openly explored as part of education. One of the reasons for this is that preventing misuse of the telekinetic powers that we cultivate in children also requires preventing the formation of unconscious repression.

From the earliest childhood, the practice of dreamwork is one method for integrating the subconscious with the conscious mind as fully as possible. Telekinesis is a predominately unconscious psychic function and can only be used in a conscious and controlled manner with a lot of training. Thus, what was once considered a normal barrier between the conscious and subconscious mind has to actually be dismantled so as to ensure that even repressed desires or malevolent intentions do not wind up being telekinetically directed at others. The most common form of repression is sexual repression. At least, it had been. The link between sexual complexes beginning in puberty and unconscious telekinesis of the type involved in poltergeist incidents or inadvertent fire-starting was observed even in the early days of parapsychological research.

Consequently, young men are sexually trained by older women, and young women by older men, who are adept at Alchemical or Tantric sex. If, in the course of the training, it comes out that a student has lesbian or gay proclivities, then she or he is also assigned a secondary trainer of the same sex. By the time this training is complete, at the end of the teenage years, a person is left with absolutely no sexual hang-ups or inhibitions. So long as it is consensual, and does not involve evident harm to others, every taboo has been broken. (Teenagers, with the kind of reason and conscience cultivated by our system of early education, are certainly considered capable of consent.)

Among the most basic of these broken taboos are the traditional attitudes toward public nudity and sex in the public sphere. In our society, fashion is exquisitely fascinating and has been transformed by metamaterials and smart paint as well as nanotechnological jewelry. The baroquely goth but colorful, and frankly Satanic, aesthetic of these clothes and accoutrements defy the old gender distinctions between masculine and feminine fashion. These clothes, which are capable of shifting shape, color, and texture, are no longer designed with a view to modesty. What parts of the body they cover and leave exposed are left entirely to the individual's eclectic aesthetic sensibilities. One often sees exposed breasts and genitals and, depending on the milieu, some people just go about naked or wearing only smart body paint. There is also plenty of sex in public places. People look at it no differently from how passionately kissing couples or wrestling friends used to be seen in public parks. The wide-eyed and childlike hybrids seem to take a somewhat perverse, voyeuristic pleasure in watching these scenes. But nobody really minds that. Although they are certainly sexual beings, their androgynous bodies with ambiguous genitalia are much slighter and more ethereal than ours and so it appears that they like to telepathically experience the sensations of more animalistic human sex. Some of them are intrigued enough by this that they seek out sexual liaisons with more prototypical humans, exercising a strangely captivating power of seduction over the latter.

Polyamory is encouraged from puberty onward, and long-term monogamy is seen as unhealthy on account of the potentially violent possessiveness and resentment that is almost inevitably tied up with it. As for marriage, it no longer exists in our society. There is a strong social support network for raising children when they are not in school. The birth mother that one has chosen remains an important person in the life of any child, but not in the context of a nuclear family with only one father or a second mother.

Not everyone chooses to be born and to go through childhood again. Many people in our society prefer to be grown as adults. These individuals opt to transfer their consciousness into fully grown replacement bodies. These may be clones of themselves or bodies genetically designed to other specifications. Training to effectively navigate the bardo state (post-mortem out-of-body experience) is part of the technique for carrying out such a transfer. The hybrids, who were all grown in this manner after the termination of the abductee-based breeding program, were forerunners in this methodology and helped more ordinary humans learn how to master it. Those who do choose to be born have to select their future mother before being reincarnated.

Both the person being reborn and the prospective mother have to undergo preparation for this directed metempsychosis. If a soul from outside interferes or tries to get into the selected mother's womb, there are techniques and technologies that can detect this so that the fetus can be aborted. Children's spontaneous early life memories of past incarnations are encouraged, not suppressed.

The Spectral Revolution has come to fruition in every dimension of its implications, from socio-political to scientific. Psi abilities, augmented by cybernetic technology, are widely used for a variety of purposes, from telekinetic healing to precognitive disaster avoidance. One of the most interesting applications has been in communication with whales, dolphins, and octopuses. These highly intelligent species were also highly responsive to telepathic attempts to enter into a dialogue with them. This predominantly took place in our colonies in the outlaw oceans of Earth, beyond the effective jurisdiction of the United Nations. But after initial successes there, we even arranged to transport significant numbers of them to our asteroid belt and Oort Cloud bases.

One of the cutting-edge frontiers of scientific research today is comprehension of the structure of the consciousness of these species. But they are not just laboratory specimens. They are being integrated into our Promethean society, which for this reason as well is rapidly becoming trans- or post-human. Our architectural spaces are being modified to accommodate them. Swimming with whales and dolphins, and conversing with them telepathically, is now a common experience, including for children. The prospect of genetically engineering human-dolphin hybrids has become a serious subject of discussion in the techno-scientific community, a discussion that has included extensive consultation with dolphins themselves. They seem to be in favor.

On account of their dexterity, octopuses, in particular, have demonstrated astonishing abilities to interact with the environment and with people through the use of technology. They freely roam in places that feature indoor waterfalls, pools, and other waterworks, including in restaurants, where they are no longer a menu item. They are not eaten by us now; they eat with us. Their precognitive abilities have been tested and proven to be so tremendous that some of them even sit on advisory councils, communicating their predictions and projections to the council members through an adept telepath trained in the linguistics of symbolic imagery. They volunteer this advice freely and find their work with us engaging. They seem to get along particularly well with the hybrids, who sometimes act as interpreters on their behalf.

No one in our society does any work that they do not love. As could already be surmised from my remarks above regarding our achievement of an economy and industry of abundance through the use of Singularity-level technologies, we have totally eliminated drudgery. A plethora of multifarious robots and AI do all of the work that no person prefers to do, and they do this work powered by free and clean Zero Point Energy. The conventional conception of labor has been replaced with passion for a vocation. Well, for a variety of vocations, either simultaneously or successively pursued. Given the increase of the human lifespan to nearly a thousand years by means of genetic engineering, not to mention the cybernetic repair of bodies at a nano-molecular level, we can expect each individual to pursue many "careers."

There are huge opportunities for "work" in the areas of archeology, anthropology, and history, now that tens of thousands of years of hitherto hidden human history have been unsealed. It is not as if the Olympians simply handed over accurate historical records of this period. That would not have been to their benefit with a view to imposing a Traditionalist quasi-feudal state on Terrestrial humanity. Nor do we want to be unquestioningly dependent on what the Ashuras have agreed to share with us as part of their ever-deepening integration into our Promethean society. We want to put it together ourselves, since every narrative of the past is written with a view to a people's future.

Another ever-expanding frontier is xenobiological epidemiology. All of the known diseases to which humans were prone back on Earth, both hereditary and epidemic, have already been eliminated from our entire population by biotechnology. However, working in space brings with it potential exposure to all kinds of alien diseases and contagions. There is also the risk that we would bring these microbes with us from the asteroid belt or the Oort Cloud to our settlements in and under Earth's oceans, thereby contaminating the entire terrestrial biosphere. So, identifying these epidemiological threats, and either eliminating them or finding a biotechnological cure for them, in advance of any potential epidemic or pandemic, is a vital mission that has elicited the passionate commitment of many biologists, geneticists, and doctors.

To my mind, the most fascinating and demanding of the fields that have emerged since the full flowering of the Spectral Revolution has been the study of the quantum computational nature of the cosmos itself. One of the most significant developments in Physics attendant to the Spectral Revolution was the recognition of free will and self-determination as part of the interaction of consciousness with the wave function on the level of quantum superposition. That put the nail in the coffin of mechanistic materialism and its deterministic — or, for that matter, purely random — account of the universe. But the question remained as to the ontological status of histories overwritten by time travelers.

What are alternate timelines, and how is it that some individuals seem to be able to pick up on fragments of them psychically? Are they really archived versions of this world or are they parallel worlds? If they are the latter, what are the implications of *that* for free will? Even if the parallel worlds are finite and accessible, rather than the infinity of "many worlds" as per the old Everett-Wheeler interpretation of Quantum Theory, that would have left no room for human agency and personal responsibility. These are also questions that have demanded the interdisciplinary collaboration of physicists and sociologists. The ethics of time travel, whether by purely technological means or through psychical techniques, poses the greatest problem for our sociologists.

The increasingly interdisciplinary character of scientific research is another achievement of the Spectral Revolution. The relationship between the various sciences is now integral and interpenetrating, not hierarchical. The superhuman data analysis capacities of Artificial Intelligence have offset the need for specialization for the sake of the focused formulation of hypotheses and testing of theories. Scientists no longer need to work in informational silos in order to get anything done. Beyond interdisciplinary collaboration amongst the sciences, the broader domain of science itself is no longer conceived of as separable from spirituality and politics. Far from being a politicization of science, or science becoming theocratic in the way that Auguste Comte envisioned, what this really means is that we no longer labor under the delusion of scientific "objectivity."

We know that power relations and spiritual aspirations cannot be filtered out of scientific research and theorization. So, instead, we have fostered a post-paradigmatic science, wherein multiple paradigms are allowed to address different practical challenges to which each of them is most suited. We do this without demanding that there be any overarching and logically consistent epistemic framework that would "reflect reality" by encompassing these paradigms and the theories that are made possible by the hinge propositions of each of them. This rejection of the idea (or idealization) of science as a mirror to Reality in favor of a view of science as a model-building endeavor with an ultimately pragmatic purpose has been the greatest achievement of the Spectral Revolution on a theoretical level. It has revolutionized the conception of "the scientific method."

This ruthlessly pragmatic or radically empirical shift toward epistemological anarchism is consistent with the anarchic nature of our society as it has developed in Earth's oceans, the asteroid belt, and the Oort Cloud. It is a society with no "laws." That also means that no one has any "rights." What we have are protocols for better rather than worse ways of accomplishing anything. Protocols are ways that things are best done. These are subject to revision and reconsideration based on experience. But the notion of civil law, as opposed to the rites and customs of archaic societies, is an idea that took shape based on the belief that "natural law" had been discovered. Such "natural law" is also the indispensable precondition for framing "rights."

Something is a human or civil "right" only when it is given by nature, not by a government that can take it away just as readily as that government granted it to the citizen. What governments give and take are duties and licenses, not to say "liberties" because liberty is also only something that a government can recognize or disregard—but never something it can give a person. The degree of liberties that exist in a society is a reflection of the degree to which a free-spirited ethos has been fostered in the individuals who constitute that society. To frame this in terms of "rights" and to make "laws" on this basis is to endorse the old conception of "natural law" that has been totally destroyed by the Spectral Revolution.

There are no laws in nature, only tendencies and habits. Even gravity is not a law. All things being equal, nothing ever has to obey a "law" of gravity. For example, Psychokinesis could supervene on the momentum of an object, and the psychological factors that then become involved do not, *in principle*, admit to mathematical calculation and projection. The concept of "law" was extrapolated out of arithmetical and geometrical tautologies in order to answer a deep psychological and social need of humans confronted with dangerous uncertainty and potentially violent instability.

Benighted Terrans living under the Olympian Order exasperatedly asked the question of how one can even run a society without laws. "What if someone commits a crime?" But what is a "crime" really? Nothing should be a crime unless it involves a harmful betrayal of one's fellows and is in some way detrimental to society. If and when someone should do such a thing, there is a protocol for dealing with it, just as there are protocols for everything else. That protocol is not about "punishing" someone for some "crime" as if the latter were a "sin." If a person does something problematic, or if the person himself becomes problematic, there are ways of dealing with the problem, and depending on what the problem is, different people are delegated to deal with it in whatever way has been determined to be most effective. But the real failure here would have been a failure in the educational and enculturation system. Laws do not produce ethical behavior.

Ethos is cultivated through one's upbringing. This becomes most clear in cases involving harm caused by misuse of psi abilities. No law can prevent this, because no legal system would be able to effectively prosecute someone for a "crime" involving misuse of ESP and telekinesis to harm another person or a group of people. Such transgressions against the autonomy of other individuals can only be prevented by fostering the development of free-spirited persons who each have profound respect and care for the other.

The real purpose of a legal order is to endow certain people with the power to punish others and to make de facto exceptions to the law for some. It is about power. But in a society where no one wants for anything, where every need is met, and where each person is provided with the education and opportunity to pursue anything that she can dream of doing, who would want to commit a crime or wield punitive power over those who do? In our society, both criminality and the lust for power are met not with the reaction that the person exhibiting them is "evil" but simply with the disgustedly dismayed question, "What is *wrong* with you?"

We have such advanced technology for repairing physical damage to people, and even resurrecting them from death, that recourse for harm done by one member of society to another is less about retribution than it is about redressing whatever profound psychological problems led to it and remedying the failure of early education to have dealt with them effectively. Of course, there is a stigma to becoming a person who merits this kind of special treatment, and, really, that is punishment enough in a society that is otherwise so tightly knit by goodwill, interpersonal trust, and authentic openness. Such transgressions are not a question of someone having broken "the law" but of someone having broken the social trust, which is infinitely worse.

Now it must be said that there is one arena in which orders are given and are expected to be followed, and where disobedience is dealt with rapidly and harshly. But, again, this is not about "law." Rather, it is a question of the chain of command. I am talking about our military. In fact, it is precisely because we have no government that the highest-ranking leader of our society is simply referred to by the title "Admiral," rather than President, Prime Minister, Chancellor, or Your Majesty. The supreme Admiral of our space navy is the commander-in-chief of the force tasked with defending our society, from the oceans of Earth to the asteroid belt and Oort Cloud. He or she is the sovereign of the Promethean world, but this sovereignty is tactical and operational. Not something written into a legal constitution. "Admiral" Hyrcanius is less a title that I hold than it is a burdensome responsibility that few would want to bear.

Moreover, while everyone in our society (irrespective of gender) receives military training from adolescence through their teenage years, actual service in the military is not compulsory. It is an all-volunteer force. We are never short of volunteers, though, and we have been on a war footing for our entire history. I suppose there is something to be said for the Olympian critique that we are able to get away with having no laws only because our society tacitly functions in a perpetual state of martial law. But martial law is usually associated with repression and scarcity, and it would be a very odd form of martial law that affords those living under it with such liberties and abundance as the members of our society enjoy.

I would say it is less martial "law" than it is the unwritten order that abides on the ships and colonies of pirates who have been tremendously successful and who are loyal to their captains and the admiral of their fleet. Now, this loyalty could, in practice, fail if, at any time, these leaders were to prove no longer competent or worthy of command. But that is also true of political leaders within the context of any constitutional regime. It is not as if laws prevent coups and revolutions from taking place.

The "law" concept is a machination of the subconscious to banish chaos. Chaos may be Pandora's box, but at the bottom of that box is hope itself. Chaos cannot be fully comprehended or encompassed by the calculative net of instrumental rationality. Chaos is that incalculable and seething abyss of dark energy that affords us an inexhaustible potential for new forms of order. Without chaos, creativity would eventually come to an end, and over a long enough span of cosmic time all forms would repeat themselves as if they were always fated to manifest as they did. In that case, their novelty would have been dispelled as a mirage of unknowing, and none of them could rightly be considered the outcome of anyone's creative act. The notions of genius and of imagination itself would be rendered absurd. Of course, that is just what the Olympians *do believe*. Despite their pretension of being "gods," they remain children frightened by that darkness from out of which our Promethean fire fearlessly blazes.

CHAPTER 5

SPACE AMAZONS

OUR WAR WITH the Olympians was not waged solely in terms of conventional military confrontation or even armed special operations. Psychological operations or psychical warfare factored into our strategy with at least equal importance. This is actually where we wound up having an advantage over their old Ashura enemies. There were more of us, and many of our people had worked to become adept psychics, having trained astral projection, among other forms of Extrasensory Perception (ESP) and Psychokinesis (PK, Telekinesis). We developed an entire corps of psychic adepts within our piratical space navy, both men and women, as well as some beautiful transsexual hermaphrodites, whose sole purpose was to use astral projection and materialization (essentially psychic or telekinetic teleportation) in order to seduce Olympian women and men in the subterranean cities of Mars. We chose the Olympians on Mars because the planet was desolate; they were far fewer in number and not surrounded by the psychic noise of the hundreds of millions of humans that they governed back on Earth.

This corps of psychic seducers effectively became incubi and succubi, tempting the self-styled "goddesses" and "gods" of Martian Olympus to deviant corruption. We considered this a more powerful vector of attack than to attempt to psychically terrorize them. The greatest terror for such totalitarians, hellbent on maintaining their poised control over everything, would, after all, be to unlock the un-fathomable abyss of repressed desires within each of them. Besides, they would likely band together to fortify their minds against any terrifying projections that we sent their way. So, instead of confront-ing them with the monstrous and eliciting a collective response, we picked them apart privately with seductions that they would never want to confess to one another.

Our psychic soldiers would telepathically explore the minds of their targets, looking for kinks that were repressed in order to ab-sorb their individuality into the collectivist and almost hive-minded organic state of the Olympians. Considering that each of them had a lifespan of thousands of years in any given body and that each had been reincarnated — or rather, resurrected in a freshly grown clone — more times than we could count or trace, this was quite a challenge. But we found these kinks and drove a wedge into them. It was different depending on the individual, and this is precisely what we were banking on. However, there were general types of repressed deviance as well.

For some, it was simply homosexual or bisexual tendencies (Olympian society, as a paragon for Terran Traditionalism, was strictly heterosexual). For others, it was to dominate a sex slave, de-livering oneself over to a frenzy of sadistic passion, or what was even more shameful for an Olympian, the secret desire to lose control by being masochistically dominated and sexually humiliated. We even exploited the longing that some of them had for sexual intimacy with children. Our psychic soldiers could retrieve their self-image from childhood as a template for crafting the appearance of the body being astral-projected to materialize in a bedchamber on Mars. We also used some of the hybrids for this purpose, albeit with their full consent. (Actually, some of them were disturbingly enthusiastic vol-unteers for this.) In this respect, having long confronted and come to terms with all of the shadows lurking in humanoid minds, we were strong, and the Olympians, with all of their repressive self-deception, were vulnerable to our machinations.

We began this project in the 2060s in the asteroid belt, and we found that, as we expanded into colonization of the Oort Cloud comets in the 2070s, the vastly increased distance to the targets was immaterial in the efficacy of the psychical operations. Of course, this was entirely consistent with the data of remote viewing and remote influencing operations carried out by the superpowers of the twentieth century against one another. But it was dramatic to see this finding hold up in principle on such a large scale. Some of our Oort Cloud colonies were more than a light year from Mars, as compared to the relative proximity of an asteroid settlement such as Ceres or Vesta. In any case, by the late 2070s, we had succeeded in sowing a deep dissonance and dissociation in these Martian minds. The Olympians stationed on Earth, or its Moon, began to notice this in their interactions with their Martian counterparts. We had to act before they figured out what was going on.

At the height of the distraction, dissension, and disarray caused by our subconscious infiltration of their society, which had yielded recriminations and persecutions, we launched a full-scale military assault on Mars. Our forces confused the Olympian fleet by coming in from three different directions. We divided their fleet with our armadas from the asteroid belt and from our rebel strongholds on Earth, while a stealth strike force sent from the Oort Cloud colonies actually landed at the entry points to the underground complexes in Cydonia and Elysium.

We were not coming to kill the Olympians. We were coming to "liberate" them. This is a seed that, over the preceding two decades, we had succeeded in planting in so many of the Martian minds that we raped into an openness to revolt against the repression of their society. Others, whose minds were more armored and with whom we had been less successful, were shocked and appalled at how their comrades seemed to lack the will to resist our assault more than half-heartedly.

The subterranean cities of Mars fell to us. Not without significant casualties, but still, it was a victory that we could never have achieved without the use of such radically asymmetrical warfare.

We delivered on our promise of "liberation," too, as we stripped our Martian captives of their last shreds of dignity and decorum. I suppose you could call it the victory of Venus over Mars. Even the Ashuras blushed at the lengths that we went to, fearing that perhaps we might someday do the same to them and realizing that they were not as free from shame as they imagined themselves to be. Those few Olympians who still had their wits about them after the orgy of sex and violence that re-consecrated the megalithic walls of those underground Martian cities with blood and cum became collaborators who facilitated our next mission: the attack on Earth's Moon and our seizure of what we came to call "Artemis Station."

We received a great deal of tactical information from them, which helped us to coordinate the operation. As I mentioned at the outset, this monumental mission took place in 2082. It began with a massive missile barrage that pulverized the regolith and blew what was taken to be "the Moon" off the metallic spherical structure orbiting the Earth. Then, with detailed schematics having been delivered to us by the Martian collaborators, which the Ashuras also helped us to interpret, we sent armed surveillance drones into the space station with a view to producing holographic films of as much of the interior as possible. These films were shown to the Terran population by every means of illicit distribution and pirate broadcasting at our disposal. Together with the imagery, we conveyed a full explanation of the archontic purpose of the exposed psychotronic machinery and the machinations for which the Grays that were manufactured inside "the Moon" had been used for millennia. Namely, to capture and control souls who would otherwise have been reincarnating more freely and deliberatively. Then we reprogrammed the Grays and threw a monkey wrench in these spectral machines.

From that decisive battle onward, the Olympians were defensively waging a losing war. Having seized from them both the cities of Mars and Artemis Station, while gaining converts and collaborators from among their ranks along the way, the Olympians were left only with their underground and undersea bases on Earth. Their control of the United Nations began to falter. Following the disclosure of the psychotronic machinations that they had secretly been using the Moon for, and which they had taken great care to continue to hide after their takeover in 2048, even the most Traditionalist Terrans within the United Nations regime turned against the Olympians. Now, there were also Traditionalist territories outside the jurisdiction of the UN, such as the Europa Group and the American Confederacy. Unlike Iran, which had left the UN over its Perennialist discourse, these were territories that remained independent because the UN was not Traditionalist *enough* for them. But as much as we would never be able to persuade them to join our cause, even these most regressive elements of the human population were sickened by what we revealed about the so-called gods, angels, or ancestors.

Some of them were pagans, whether the Odinists of Europa or the Vedic Indians; others were adherents of various forms of Abrahamic orthodoxy that had compelled them to resist the UN, however Traditionalist its own discourse eventually became. The latter ran the whole gamut from Evangelical Americans to Sunni Muslims. As for the ancestor-worshippers, namely the Chinese Confucianists with their collectivist mentality, they *had* largely accepted the UN system, since China was the de facto leader of it. But whatever differences existed amongst these groups, one common denominator was certainly Patriarchy. That the Universal Declaration of Human Rights was no guarantee against the subordination of women had already become clear in the early twentieth century, when countries such as Saudi Arabia were allowed not only to sit on the UN Human Rights Council but to chair it. As for those ultra-Traditionalist populations in regions of America, Europe, and the Middle East that had left the UN when it transformed into a putative World Government, they were even more unequivocally patriarchal in their social structure. Consequently, as the paternalistic hold of the Olympians over these Traditionalist populations weakened, and as they were thrown into a state of confusion by what we had revealed about Earth's overlords, we decided to make Patriarchy our primary target in the final phase of our war with Olympus. Here, also, psychological warfare would be paramount in our strategy for victory.

As I have recounted, our Promethean society had surmounted all gender-based politics together with the psychical and technological deconstruction of limiting fixations on sexual binaries. But for the purposes of psychological operations against our Traditionalist adversaries on Earth, we decided to engineer the specter of an armed force commanded entirely by women. We recruited these Space Amazons not only from out of our standing military, and especially from its special forces, but also asked for volunteers from the general population of women who were both motivated and fit enough to be trained for this operation. As I explained earlier, everyone in our society grew up with a physical education regimen that included martial arts, gymnastics, and Yoga, and then also underwent basic military training. So, the baseline of competence was already rather high, at least compared to the benighted population back on Earth.

Genetic enhancement and cybernetic augmentation were also factors in this. We had eliminated the physical gap between women and men in terms of stature, strength, and endurance. In our Promethean society, these qualities now varied more from individual to individual than they did between the sexes. In other words, those Promethean women who were engaged in sports — let alone those already serving in our military — were larger and stronger than most men back on Earth, except for the ones in our ocean-based colonies and in Greater Iran, which was fully integrated into the Promethean community of the asteroid belt and the Oort Cloud. There was a certain historical justice to this, too, since Iran was the homeland of the

Amazons. Or, rather, of the actual historical people that the patriarchal Greeks — who were terrified of them — referred to as "Amazons."
I mean the Scythians and, even more so, the Sarmatians, who were
closely related to them and are often conflated with them.

In the first of these two groups of northern Iranian barbarians,
women fought alongside men as horseback archers, and they were
headstrong enough to have sex with whomever they wanted without
asking the permission of their husbands. The men who tolerated this
were far from cuckold sissies. Actually, they were the fiercest fight-
ers of the entire ancient world — the original berserkers, even more
ferocious than later Norse and Celtic barbarians. These were men who
mixed the blood of their slain enemies with amanita-spiked wine and
drank it from out of chalices that they had fashioned from the skulls
of the vanquished. Their spears were decorated with trophy scalps.
Now and then, they were even ruled by a queen instead of a king, the
most infamous of them being Queen Tomyris, who defeated Cyrus
the Great in battle before decapitating him and plunging his severed
head into her wineskin. The Scythian war banner was the wolf's head.

As for the Sarmatians, they were an altogether matriarchal society.
Putting the lie to gender stereotypes, they were also the most advanced
warrior society of their epoch. Although known for their unsurpassed
skill in archery and horseback riding, they were also the first people of
the post-Atlantean epoch to forge and wield *iron* swords. In fact, the
word *iron* comes from their language, in which it is their pronuncia-
tion of the name "Iran" or Aryan. They invented scale armor, which
they not only wore as body armor but also draped over their horses.
The striking impression that this scale armor made on the terrified
ancient Greek men who fought them must at least in part have accounted for their name having been warped to *Sauromatae* in Greek,
meaning "reptilians" (the same *saur* as in dinosaur). Surely, it did not
help that the standard they carried into battle was a serpentine, scaly,
winged dragon.

Their actual name, in Old Iranian, was *Sarmat*, or "the people of the cold." They descended into the Black Sea region from out of the snowy Caucasus Mountains, eventually stretching to Western Anatolia, where they built the original temple of Artemis at Ephesus — the one recognized as among the seven wonders of the ancient world. "Artemis," or *Artâ–Ameshâ*, was their goddess. As you may recall, in Old Iranian the name means "Immortal Truth." A somewhat paradoxical name, since the Sarmatians believed that the only eternal or undying truth about the world is that it is energy perpetually in a state of dynamic flux — which they symbolized as a fire ever-changing its forms. It was not at all incidental that the philosopher Heraclitus dedicated his writings *On Nature* to the priestesses of the Temple of Artemis, and then sequestered himself to its confines after a democratic Greek revolt brought Imperial Iranian rule to an end in his native Ephesus. Their other name for the great goddess was *Satana*, matriarch of the Gorgons, who was entwined with serpents and believed to rule an occulted realm beneath the Caspian Sea. Artemis was known in Greek as "the torch-bearing light bringer" and the "crafty infernal one." In Latin, in addition to being identified with Diana, she was also called *Lucifera*. The crescent moon, taken together with Venus or "the Morning Star," namely Lucifer, was her predominant symbol. In other words, she is the female aspect of "Satan." Occasionally, worthy men were chosen to be abducted to this undersea fortress to be initiated and trained as knights in her service.

The legend of Arthur and the Lady of the Lake was based on these Sarmatian beliefs and carried to Britain and France by "Alans," or Sarmatians, captured in battle by Caesar Marcus Aurelius, who, in his wisdom as a philosopher king, knew that they were far too valuable to kill or enslave. Instead, he integrated them into the Roman military but stationed them far from their own lands on the Empire's eastern front. Later, other "Alans" (a cognate of the Old Northwest Iranian *Arani*, or "Aryan," in a dialect where *r* turns into *l*) migrated to Europe in large numbers as part of the "barbarian invasions" of collapsing

Rome. Eventually, their descendants became the most sophisticated element of Medieval European society, with the other "barbarians" (Germans, Celts) being subordinate to them. They were responsible for the chivalric culture and grail mysticism of the land-owning noblewomen and their troubadours in Occitan — a dreaded bane of the Catholic Church and of all patriarchal and paternalistic Europeans of that age. The Holy Inquisition was invented in order to torture and burn these Europeanized Iranians into submission, and was only later applied to other religious minorities such as Jews and Muslims. This largely hidden history had finally entered the textbooks in Iran during the 2040s, so that by now two generations of Iranian women had been raised with a keen awareness of it. It was no surprise then that besides recruiting from our colonies in Earth's oceans, in the Oort Cloud and in the the asteroid belt, we had plenty of volunteers from Iran as well. Ironically, Iran became the "Great Satan" among the nations.

As our initial targets, we chose Traditionalist communities wherein we knew there was significant internal dissent. So, for example, we did not target Sunni Muslim territories in the Arab World or Africa, where women had largely accepted patriarchy as part of their own value system. Rather, we started with places like the American Confederacy. From the moment when Evangelicals seized power in that area, and then consolidated it by being the only social force capable of holding back an otherwise inevitable race war between southern blacks and whites, there had also been a fairly hardcore minority of dissenters. In fact, by 2050, the American South had become a bastion of Satanism. It was underground and only galvanized about ten percent of the population, but that minority was militant and motivated. The more fundamentalist Christianity began to rule through the state and confederate legislatures, and seize control of the courts in old Dixie, the more formerly bland secular, atheistic humanists began to become polarized in the opposite direction and rebrand themselves as outright Satanists. The mainstream scientific acceptance of Parapsychology also played a role in this since it divested the secular atheists of their materialism. Another similar target for us were the Traditionalist Catholic communities in Central and Eastern Europe, where dissent against the Church in the form of "Satanic" Sorcery and Witchcraft had a history going back to the Middle Ages. We began by breaking political prisoners out of jail and liberating those who had been incarcerated for "moral improprieties."

From Warsaw to Nashville, rumors spread about Valkyries dropping out of the sky onto penitentiary or reformatory rooftops. Those Americans and Europeans who were freed gave us vital intelligence about the subtleties of their own societies. This enabled us to design more effective strategies specific to the deconstruction of one or another Traditionalist stronghold wherein a potential fifth column of dissenters were ready and waiting to become insurgents. We employed covert operations to have our Amazons infiltrate these societies and embed themselves amongst these dissenters, together with the freed rebels who were set up in safe houses, and we trained them in various tactics of insurgency. Then, at certain optimal times when local law enforcement had its guard lowered, we would set off an armed insurgency within one or another town or small city. Once the insurgency succeeded in decapitating the local Traditionalist leadership of the community, and setting fire to churches, courthouses, and other instruments of an essentially theocratic tyranny of the majority, our Amazon army would arrive — usually from out of the sky or, in cases where it was a river town or port city that was being liberated, from out of the water.

We preferred not to carry out mass executions, but we did insist on reeducation of all of the children, teenagers, and young adults in these communities. The first thing we would do after physically securing a community would be to set up a Promethean-style school there — or in some cases, several, for all levels of general education. Many of these were akin to boarding schools with dormitories, since a significant number of kids had to be seized from regressive parents who wanted to brainwash them into Evangelical or Catholic fundamentalism. A lot of the youths were suffering from Stockholm syndrome, but we eventually awed them with technological wonders that had been hidden from them and we psychically let loose all that their elders had repressed in them. It did not take long for many of the girls to want to grow up to become like the Space Amazons that walked amongst them, or for as many of the boys to be driven mad with desire for these harsh and otherworldly mistresses. If they could not scheme their way into getting lucky with one of these Valkyries, they at least wanted to be roughed up by one occasionally. As the black flag of Prometheism rose over each liberated town and city, spreading like a firestorm, it had an evocatively erotic power that transcended the political. It was a talisman. A dark sigil.

Once news of our rebellions in non-UN territories reached the few remaining large cities of Earth, all of which — with the exception of those in Iran, of course — were run by the United Nations, we dealt the death blow. As I mentioned earlier, following our attack on the Moon and our exposure of what the Olympians had been using the space station for, there had been an anti-Olympian coup within the United Nations leadership. Instead of embracing this coup and its leaders, who wanted us to accept the UN system and integrate ourselves into it, we launched a devastating strike on the UN Headquarters at the Palais des Nations in Geneva, as well as a dozen other leading UN institutions in other cities, such as UNESCO in Paris. We then forced the metropolitan populations, who had seen what we were already accomplishing with our Amazon army in the Traditionalist hinterlands, to choose either unmediated Olympian rule over them or unconditional surrender to the Promethean space navy.

The humane buffer of the UN was gone. They would have to choose between an outright caste system governed by the "gods" or bear the burden of being freed by us from their own deep desire to be slaves. The decision was made pretty clearly across former civilizational lines, with the last remaining metropolises of the old Western World, the most prominent of which was Paris, choosing to join Iran as part of the solar-system-wide Promethean community and the non-Western lands looking to their Hindu gods, Abrahamic angels, and Confucian ancestors to save them from what they feared most: freedom.

Not everyone in the West embraced Prometheism, of course. Rather, people from a whole variety of religions and ideologies were invited to be a part of our community without necessarily considering themselves Prometheists. These included 'Christian' Gnostics, radically antinomian 'Sufis' and Nizari Ismailis, Theosophists, Thelemites, Taoists, practitioners of Tantra, Buddhists, especially of the Vajrayana and Zen varieties, Solarpunks, Lunarpunks, Chaos Magicians, Wiccans, and wide varieties of Satanists whose focus was on some Satanic archetype other than Prometheus (the Setians, for example). The term "Counter-Traditional" would best encompass all of these disparate rebels against the Traditionalist world order, who accepted the protection and leadership of Prometheism while continuing to adhere to their own beliefs. We all stood together as a rebel alliance against what was left of the World of Tradition ruled by the Devas. With the world divided along these lines, we played our end game. Or, rather, I should say with the Earth divided along these lines, because by this point the rest of the solar system was ours.

The reptilians harbored a profound resentment and hatred of humanity as a whole, but they had developed a modus vivendi with the Ashuras, who inhabited the same stratum of the subterranean and submarine depths of the planet as they did. In this case, the enemy of their enemy certainly could not be counted as a "friend," but, nonetheless, it was the Olympians or Devas who had genetically engineered the reptilians as a slave race of dinosaur-human hybrids. It was the Devas who, after rejecting and abandoning this species of "dragons," made a sport and a heroic rite of passage out of hunting and slaying them. It was the Devas who, after the Ashuras waged a revolutionary war against them on Mars, decided to break their temporal quarantine by terraforming and colonizing an Earth still dominated by dinosaurs. An act which resulted in a re-writing of the timeline, such that a particular species of dinosaur, namely the Troodon, would no longer naturally evolve into a humanoid form and develop an advanced technical culture. The asteroid impact in the Yucatan 65 million years ago was directed by these Nordic time travelers. It was also at that time that they parked what became Earth's "Moon" in orbit in order to reshape the entire terrestrial biosphere with a view to human habitation.

The paradox of how and whether humans would have evolved in the first place, had this not taken place, was still a subject of philosophical debate. The Olympians wanted to believe that, in a time loop that they wore as a ring of divine authority, they were always destined to be the creators of themselves — namely of the Nordic Master Race — and, by extension, of the rest of humanity. The Ashuras took a different position. So did the reptilians, who felt that their legitimate future history had been stolen from them, when, instead of evolving as a proud and free race in their own right, their genetic predecessors were hybridized with human genes to engineer slaves for hard labor, such as in mines.

Following a revolt against their slave masters and their breakaway into a subterranean and submarine civilization of their own, the reptilians had learned how to synthesize DMT. They used it in such a way as they were afforded access to a parallel world wherein their species, or one very similar to it, had become the dominant race on Earth rather than Homo Sapiens, which had never evolved on that world line. They had met with some success in opening a portal through which these otherworldly and more advanced, space-faring reptilians could access our reality.

Together with the Ashuras, we approached the reptilians with an offer. We would allow them to emerge from their lairs deep beneath the Earth's mantle and use our territory as a staging ground for a massive assault on those regions, mostly in (what had formerly been) the Eastern hemisphere, that were dominated by Traditionalists still loyal to the Olympian overlords. We would feed these "gods" and their mindless minions to the reptilians, allowing their race to colonize and populate large parts of a planet that, in one very possible future, would have been theirs anyhow. They would serve as eaters of the dead, of those who had decided against the evolutionary force of life and the Promethean will of the *Aion*.

We knew that we could count on the mantids, who were brought here from Earth's far future (well, from *a* potentially overwritten future) by the cephalopod superorganism that had reached back across geological and anthropological history through spatiotemporal vortices in the oceans. The mantids were definitely a match for the reptilians. Between them, the hybrids, which they helped to create, our own post-Singularity society, the battle-hardened Ashuras, and those android Grays that we had reprogrammed after seizing them on Artemis Station, we could reasonably expect that the reptilians would not be able to overstep the bounds of our agreement with them. Meanwhile, the mantids, who were masters of hybridization, including in a shamanic spiritual sense, set about developing reptilian-human hybrids (the reptilians were, of course, already partly human hybrids themselves). This hybridized population would serve as a biological and cultural bridge to the reptilian society on the other side of the planet and to the more advanced inter-dimensional reptilians who had begun to integrate with them.

It is worthy of note that, as part of this hybridization program, some of our Amazon soldiers volunteered as the mates of male reptilians and the mothers of the "dragon-bloods" that were technologically helped in being born from these unions. Whereas the reptilians had been accustomed to brutally raping the human women that they had occasionally abducted over the centuries and millennia, in the context of this program and under the stewardship of the mantids, the Amazons were always in a sexually dominant position with regard to the reptilian males who had been designated to be a part of this project. Ironically, "Sarmatian" would, in a sense, come to have the meaning attributed to the word by the ancient Greeks.

Those who valorized the symbol of the pyramid and whose hierarchical world order had for so long been based on inhumane oppression and slavish submissiveness were devoured by masters more cold-blooded than they could have imagined. Those who had fed off the energy of human souls from that fortress once known as the Moon were now food for the rejuvenation of the dying dragon race. Our loyalty was never to humanity but rather to the revolutionary force of cosmic evolution and to all those, of all species, who also align themselves with it — with He/r. Human, mantid, reptilian — S/he wears the beauty of every race as a dancing shaman's mask. With Artemis unveiled, He/r time has come. Her *aeon*. The Prometheaion.

OTHER BOOKS PUBLISHED BY ARKTOS

SRI DHARMA PRAVARTAKA ACHARYA	*The Dharma Manifesto*
JOAKIM ANDERSEN	*Rising from the Ruins*
WINSTON C. BANKS	*Excessive Immigration*
ALAIN DE BENOIST	*Beyond Human Rights*
	Carl Schmitt Today
	The Ideology of Sameness
	The Indo-Europeans
	Manifesto for a European Renaissance
	On the Brink of the Abyss
	The Problem of Democracy
	Runes and the Origins of Writing
	View from the Right (vol. 1–3)
ARMAND BERGER	*Tolkien, Europe, and Tradition*
ARTHUR MOELLER VAN DEN BRUCK	*Germany's Third Empire*
MATT BATTAGLIOLI	*The Consequences of Equality*
KERRY BOLTON	*The Perversion of Normality*
	Revolution from Above
	Yockey: A Fascist Odyssey
ISAC BOMAN	*Money Power*
CHARLES WILLIAM DAILEY	*The Serpent Symbol in Tradition*
RICARDO DUCHESNE	*Faustian Man in a Multicultural Age*
ALEXANDER DUGIN	*Ethnos and Society*
	Ethnosociology
	Eurasian Mission
	The Fourth Political Theory
	The Great Awakening vs the Great Reset
	Last War of the World-Island
	Political Platonism
	Putin vs Putin
	The Rise of the Fourth Political Theory
	The Theory of a Multipolar World
EDWARD DUTTON	*Race Differences in Ethnocentrism*
MARK DYAL	*Hated and Proud*
CLARE ELLIS	*The Blackening of Europe*
KOENRAAD ELST	*Return of the Swastika*
JULIUS EVOLA	*The Bow and the Club*
	Fascism Viewed from the Right
	A Handbook for Right-Wing Youth
	Metaphysics of Power
	Metaphysics of War
	The Myth of the Blood
	Notes on the Third Reich
	The Path of Cinnabar
	Recognitions
	A Traditionalist Confronts Fascism

OTHER BOOKS PUBLISHED BY ARKTOS

GUILLAUME FAYE	*Archeofuturism*
	Archeofuturism 2.0
	The Colonisation of Europe
	Convergence of Catastrophes
	Ethnic Apocalypse
	A Global Coup
	Prelude to War
	Sex and Deviance
	Understanding Islam
	Why We Fight
DANIEL S. FORREST	*Suprahumanism*
ANDREW FRASER	*Dissident Dispatches*
	Reinventing Aristocracy in the Age of Woke Capital
	The WASP Question
GÉNÉRATION IDENTITAIRE	*We are Generation Identity*
PETER GOODCHILD	*The Taxi Driver from Baghdad*
	The Western Path
PAUL GOTTFRIED	*War and Democracy*
PETR HAMPL	*Breached Enclosure*
PORUS HOMI HAVEWALA	*The Saga of the Aryan Race*
LARS HOLGER HOLM	*Hiding in Broad Daylight*
	Homo Maximus
	Incidents of Travel in Latin America
	The Owls of Afrasiab
RICHARD HOUCK	*Liberalism Unmasked*
A. J. ILLINGWORTH	*Political Justice*
ALEXANDER JACOB	*De Naturae Natura*
JASON REZA JORJANI	*Closer Encounters*
	Faustian Futurist
	Iranian Leviathan
	Lovers of Sophia
	Novel Folklore
	Prometheism
	Promethean Pirate
	Prometheus and Atlas
	Uber Man
	World State of Emergency
HENRIK JONASSON	*Sigmund*
EDGAR JULIUS JUNG	*The Significance of the German Revolution*
RUUBEN KAALEP & AUGUST MEISTER	*Rebirth of Europe*
RODERICK KAINE	*Smart and SeXy*
PETER KING	*Here and Now*
	Keeping Things Close
	On Modern Manners
JAMES KIRKPATRICK	*Conservatism Inc.*

OTHER BOOKS PUBLISHED BY ARKTOS

LUDWIG KLAGES — *The Biocentric Worldview*
Cosmogonic Reflections
The Science of Character

ANDREW KORYBKO — *Hybrid Wars*

PIERRE KREBS — *Guillaume Faye: Truths & Tributes*
Fighting for the Essence

JULIEN LANGELLA — *Catholic and Identitarian*

JOHN BRUCE LEONARD — *The New Prometheans*

STEPHEN PAX LEONARD — *The Ideology of Failure*
Travels in Cultural Nihilism

WILLIAM S. LIND — *Reforging Excalibur*
Retroculture

PENTTI LINKOLA — *Can Life Prevail?*

H. P. LOVECRAFT — *The Conservative*

NORMAN LOWELL — *Imperium Europa*

RICHARD LYNN — *Sex Differences in Intelligence*

JOHN MACLUGASH — *The Return of the Solar King*

CHARLES MAURRAS — *The Future of the Intelligentsia &*
For a French Awakening

JOHN HARMON MCELROY — *Agitprop in America*

MICHAEL O'MEARA — *Guillaume Faye and the Battle of Europe*
New Culture, New Right

MICHAEL MILLERMAN — *Beginning with Heidegger*

MAURICE MURET — *The Greatness of Elites*

BRIAN ANSE PATRICK — *The NRA and the Media*
Rise of the Anti-Media
The Ten Commandments of Propaganda
Zombology

TITO PERDUE — *The Bent Pyramid*
Journey to a Location
Lee
Morning Crafts
Philip
The Sweet-Scented Manuscript
William's House (vol. 1–4)

JOHN K. PRESS — *The True West vs the Zombie Apocalypse*

RAIDO — *A Handbook of Traditional Living* (vol. 1–2)

CLAIRE RAE RANDALL — *The War on Gender*

STEVEN J. ROSEN — *The Agni and the Ecstasy*
The Jedi in the Lotus

NICHOLAS ROONEY — *Talking to the Wolf*

RICHARD RUDGLEY — *Barbarians*
Essential Substances
Wildest Dreams

OTHER BOOKS PUBLISHED BY ARKTOS

Made in United States
Troutdale, OR
08/09/2024

21853641R00065